A Tragic Tea Party

Wonderland Detective Agency Book 5

Jeannie Wycherley

A Tragic Tea Party
Wonderland Detective Agency Book 5
By
JEANNIE WYCHERLEY

Sign up for Jeannie's newsletter:
www.subscribepage.com/JeannieWycherleyWonky

A Tragic Tea Party was edited by Christine L Baker
Cover design by Ravenborn Covers.
Formatting by Tammy
Proofreading by Johnny Bon Bon
Please note: This book is set in England in the United Kingdom and therefore uses British English spellings and idioms throughout.

Author's Note

I owe a debt of gratitude to my wonderful street team who helped me choose some names for this story.

This book is dedicated to

Maisie Richards, Nicky Richards, Julie Dycus Smith, Suzanne Smith, Tia Michele Chandler, Jennifer Lee Munzlinger, Rhonda McLaughlin, Deborah Forrester, Debbie Napier, Jill Witowski, Pat Turner, Pascal Norbury and Mel Bolton!

With grateful thanks
Jeannie Wycherley
29th July 2022

CHAPTER 1

The streetlamp above my head fizzled and died as I drifted beneath it. Lost in thought, barely paying attention, I peered up, the light moisture of London drizzle coating the skin on my face. How that was feasible when there was barely enough room for a bird to fly between the crooked buildings either side of me, I had no idea.

My thoughts tripped over themselves. Idle. Curious. Yet fleeting. Rather like the beating of a pigeon's wings as it navigates its way to its loft.

Is London drizzle as fresh and wholesome as Devon drizzle? I doubted it. I'd spent the weekend in Exeter with George, DS Gilchrist, my sometime love. We'd driven out to the moor, where I'd stared at a landscape stunning in its rolling desolation. Miles and miles of green and brown and grey. The sky grim and foreboding, the fresh wind whipping at my hair.

Beautiful, undoubtedly. But I was no country girl. Where were all the people? All the buildings? Where was all the energy? How could George bear the quiet and solitude there?

Nonetheless, we'd enjoyed our together time, a rare enough occurrence given our busy work schedules. We'd packed a lot in—sightseeing, restaurants, even a trip to the cinema—and I'd only arrived back in Tumble Town at ten this morning after a four-hour drive. After dropping off my hire car, I'd headed directly to the Wonderland office to meet an existing client and interview several new ones. One gentleman had asked me to have his wife followed as he suspected her of having an affair with a warlock in the next street. I'd accepted the case. It would be easy enough to have Ezra Izax—my deceased partner who helped me out with my investigations—haunt the lane where they lived and observe what the wife got up to.

The second interview had been with a much older woman, well into her eighties. Having recovered—eventually—from climbing the stairs to our attic office, she confessed that she feared her housekeeper had been stealing from her for the past forty years. Little and often.

I'd stared at Ezra—who occupied the corner desk in our shared office—and he'd momentarily pursed his lips. This was a sign he thought we should take the case. The goddess alone knows why. He liked this kind of complex investigation. Plus, being a ghost really has its advantages at times. He would be able to snoop around in the house without the housekeeper knowing about it.

But then Ezra's left eye had quivered slightly. He'd decided the wealthy widow was completely barking. I had to agree. Who waits *forty years* to act on something they've suspected for so long?

Whatever. We'd taken the case.

Being 'barking', in Tumble Town, is an occupational hazard. And my Wonderland Detective Agency wasn't in the habit of declining cases just because we felt our clients were a little bit nutty. We were a business. We had bills to pay. If we declined every fruit bat who approached us, we'd be bankrupt in a few weeks.

By lunchtime, my lack of sleep had made my head ache. This had been compounded by Wizard Dodo's relentless bickering with my office manager, Wootton Fitzpaine.

Poor Wootton.

The elderly wizard, as dead as his namesake, really had it in for the youngster at times. So far, I hadn't been able to get to the bottom of the issue. But I would.

When I had a moment.

Though they were few and far between.

Eventually, after a busy but uneventful day, I'd left the office relatively early, just after half past five, imagining I'd scoot back to my apartment overlooking Peachstone Market, change into my running gear and hit the streets for thirty minutes or so while there was still some decent light left. It doesn't matter what time of the year it is in Tumble Town, night falls early because the daylight finds it impossible to steal between the cramped confines of the crowded old buildings in this paranormal enclave. Lodgings shuffle together on the edge of the Thames, becoming ever more dilapidated the deeper you venture, the inhabitants of those dwellings as ragged and woebegone as the rooms they rent, or as dark and forbidding as the alleys they meander during the midnight hours.

I wasn't averse to running at night—well, that's what I

told myself—but not being a Tumble Town native, it paid to take a little personal care and keep myself safe from the threats that roamed the alleys and back lanes seeking a little excitement and a quick buck.

Still lost in thought, I'd slowed as I entered Sneinton Shute and stepped into a doorway to allow a fellow pedestrian a little leeway. He was a big man. Tall. Broad. Robed. With the hood pulled up, I couldn't see his face. This was the Tumble Town way. No-one wanted to be seen or acknowledged. I dropped my eyes; let him pass in peace.

Pssss-sksss-psssk-hhhhusss-ssss.

Whispering at my shoulder.

Paying no attention, I stepped out onto the cobbled passageway.

Pssss-surrrusssssksss-psss-hhhhhurussssss-susss.

Thin, cold lips pressed to my ear.

"That tickles," I said, my voice loud in this narrow alley.

Psss-sksss-russ-sssskussss.

Wiggling my shoulder in annoyance, as though *that* pathetic gesture would get rid of a shadow person with no physical form, I continued on my way.

"You're going to be late."

The words in my ear, as clear as crystal, the shock of breath on my cheek with the plosive t, pulled me up short. I twisted sideways, searching for the owner of *that* male voice. *Familiar?* I questioned. *But how could that be?*

"Late," repeated another voice.

"Late."

The word echoed around me, taken up by countless others. *Late. Late. Late. Late.*

"Late for what?" I asked.

The whispers rapidly faded away, sucked into the brick stucco walls on either side of me. I should have known better than to try and engage the Shadow People in conversation.

"Hmm." Shaking my head, I turned forwards and, as I did so, the far end of the alleyway seemed to flicker, like the frames in old-fashioned black and white movies. A portal? I frowned. I'd walked this way a thousand times and never come across a portal before. There were portals the length and breadth of Tumble Town. To my limited knowledge, some of them were created as a temporary gate between here and somewhere else. I didn't understand how they worked and didn't have much experience of them at all. To me, they were something unknown. The unknown made me uneasy. I faltered, then turned back; I'd take a different route home.

But as I pivoted, the air shimmered and the damp cobbles sparkled. Five or six metres in front of me, the grime between the stones rippled and shifted. It seemed to rise, as though a giant mole was burrowing upwards, but the pile of stones and dirt continued to grow, drawn ever upwards, then finally stretching ... stretching ... and taking on a human shape with a head and legs and arms ... But only momentarily. As it lifted those arms, what should have been flesh melted and stretched like hot toffee ...

Forming wings.

I jerked backwards as the shape leapt upwards, beat its wings once then soared away, up through the tiny gap between the Elizabethan buildings that leaned in on each other.

Craning my head, struggling to catch a further glimpse,

I let out an audible gasp, unaware I'd been holding my breath. *What ...?*

I'd seen something similar once before. Not exactly the same, but almost. Back then I'd been hunting the Tweedles.

We'd never found them.

Thoroughly unnerved, I almost abandoned the idea of heading home. Wouldn't it be better to return to the office and speak to Ezra? But I was tired. Tomorrow was another day. This could wait until then.

Stuck between a rock and a hard place. Was this important or just one of those Tumble Town 'peculiarities' that I should write off? I glanced up the alley and then back behind me. Home or office? Office or home?

A run, a long hot shower and a bowl of pasta followed by an early night sounded good to me.

Torn, I watched as an elderly woman, clad in a cheap grey cloak and pulling a shopping trolley, began shuffling towards me, her back rounded and shoulders hunched. Through force of habit, I stepped into another doorway, this one shallow, pressing my spine against the door. She took her time, bless her, and as she drew closer, I heard the wheeze of her chest. No doubt decades of breathing in Tumble Town's thick, toxic air had done that to her.

Perhaps that was as good a reason as any to escape to the countryside—to George—one day in the future.

But not yet.

She drew alongside me, the wheels of her trolley scraping the cobbles, her breath exploding in dry gasps. I dropped my gaze, noted the swollen feet clad in wide beige shoes that had seen better days. Then she had passed me and the trolley rumbled on.

I'm going home, I decided, stepping out into the alley. *I've had enough for today.*

A bright white rectangle lay on the cobblestones. It hadn't been there before. I would have noticed it, so incongruous did it look, gleaming among the grime and rubbish of the alleyway. I leaned over to take a better look. An envelope.

The old lady must have been on her way to post it and dropped it.

"Excuse me!" I called back over my shoulder. "Excuse me?" I pivoted.

The old woman and her trolley had disappeared.

That just isn't possible, I told myself. *She wasn't moving fast enough to make it to the end of the lane!*

I crouched beside the envelope and reached for it. My fingers seemed to scrabble on the stones for a moment, but then I had it. Light as a feather, I could tell just from the touch of the paper on my skin that this was expensive vellum—starched and crisp and so incredibly bright. Why would an old woman who couldn't afford a decent cloak or shoes have stationery of this quality?

I could post it for her. Did it have a stamp?

I flipped the envelope over.

No address. Just a name. Scratched into the paper in a beautiful, flowing script.

Elise Liddell.

My heart performed a little one-two. *What the heck?* Stupidly, I gazed up the alley once more as though looking for her would suddenly bring the old dear back. *Why not just hand it to me?*

I smoothed the corner of the envelope where a smudge

of grime had soiled its perfection. I should open it, but suddenly felt loathe to do so.

That's crazy, I told myself. *It's addressed to me! How many other Elise Liddells are there in Tumble Town? In London? In the world?*

Standing, I moved directly under the street lamp hanging from an iron bracket fixed to the walls on either side of me. It did little to dispel the gloom, but I held the envelope up to the light and examined it from different angles. I spotted the faint outline of a watermark, little else.

Turning it over again, I slid my thumbnail under the flap in the corner and gently eased it free. No need for tearing; it came unstuck effortlessly. Inside was a single sheet of paper of the same quality as the envelope. I slipped it out and unfolded it.

The letterhead contained an embossed logo in the top right-hand corner of the sheet that jumped out at me. Engraved in green and gold was the Ministry of Witches logo, entwined with the simpler logo for the MOWPD. Directly beneath that was the name and address of The Extraordinary High Society for the Endowment of Judicial Awards.

They sounded fancy, but I'd never heard of them.

The main body of the letter was short and sweet.

Dear Ms Liddell, it read.

The Extraordinary High Society for the Endowment of Judicial Awards request the pleasure of your company at 48 Fletcher Gate at 6 pm this evening. High tea will be provided.

Yours sincerely

Underneath was a scribble that might have said anything. The name had not been typed out below.

"Huh." I turned the invitation over but there was nothing on the reverse.

There were no RSVP contact details either, and no phone number attached to the logo at the head of the page.

"For Pete's sake," I grumbled. "What is this? Why can't I just go home?" I reread the letter. How could I go looking like this? I ran a hand across my damp crown. I probably looked a right state.

"I have no idea where Fletcher Gate is," I grumbled and hooked my mobile out of my leather jacket pocket. Snitch would know. I'd give him a call.

"You're going to be late," the voice in the shadows reminded me.

"Late!" Others took up the cry. "Late!"

I thumbed the screen, searching for Snitch's number.

"For a very important date," someone hissed.

I rolled my eyes. "Get out of here!"

Chapter 2

"Are we there yet?" I asked. I didn't mean to be impatient, but my hair was plastered against my skull and the damp was beginning to seep down the neck of my jacket.

"Owww," Snitch called. "Not far now, DC Liddell."

No matter how many times I'd reminded him, Snitch could never—or would never—remember that I was a detective inspector. Not that it mattered, given I was retired. I wouldn't have minded at all if Snitch had called me Elise, as almost everyone else did these days, but he seemed to think I should be accorded a title, even if it wasn't the correct one.

He knew every rat run, did Snitch. I studied his back as he led me down a passageway that was so narrow in places I had to turn sideways to avoid my shoulder bag snagging on the rough surface of the walls. Speaking of rats, he looked like a half-drowned one tonight. Like a man who'd been out in the rain for hours. This was probably the case. He was a curious fellow. Young, mid-twenties at a push. Pale and weasel-faced with most of his teeth missing, a pointy nose and long lank hair. Yet there was something earnest and sweet about him too.

When I'd first met him—and let's for the moment skirt over the fact that I was blotto—I'd assumed he was one of Tumble Town's dubious characters who shouldn't be trusted. In fact, he'd turned out to be one of the least shady people I'd had the displeasure of meeting since moving here from the 'light' side of Celestial Street. That's not to say Snitch was squeaky clean by any means; he had many shadowy contacts that I preferred to know nothing about, and he had fingers in pies that he chose to keep secret, but he'd become a useful ally in my investigations. When I'd put him on the books of the Wonderland Detective Agency, he'd been quite overcome. It was the first time he'd drawn a salary in his life. And while it wasn't much, he was grateful for every penny.

I had no idea what he spent his money on though. The boots he was wearing were ones I'd bought for him over a year ago, and the cloak he had on had long since seen better days. Add in the fact that he rarely bothered to get his hair cut, and clearly had never been formally introduced to soap and water, and what I had here was a curious fellow to be sure.

Nowadays, he was one of the family.

"Just down here, DC Liddell," Snitch said, and squeezed out of the alley and into a wider thoroughfare.

I throw the word thoroughfare around as though we'd finally ended up on a busy road of some description. This was not the case. Fletcher Gate was wide enough for two fully laden mules to pass if they needed to, and it had enough space, in places, for the streetlamps to be free-standing rather than to hang from brackets, but other than that, it was a typical Tumble Town route—cobbled, dark, quiet.

The houses here were early Victorian: once grand structures of three or four storeys—depending on whether you included the servants' quarters at the top—with sash windows and short flights of stone steps leading to wide front doors complete with brass furnishings.

Once upon a time, these would have been dwellings for the well-to-do. Now every one of them seemed lonely and forlorn, neglected by successive owners and those who rented the rooms inside each building. The paintwork flaked, windows were cracked, net curtains were torn and filthy, drainpipes hung loose, and one or two had been daubed with graffiti.

Except, as I peered down the street, I knew exactly which house number 48 would be. It had to be the one that glowed with light. I'd seen movies where balls were being held at wonderful mansions, and as the carriages pulled up and the women in their bell-shaped dresses were helped to the ground by their charming beaus, the candlelight would spill out of every window and you would feel the excitement of the partygoers. This house gave off that sort of energy. As we strolled closer and I began to rummage in my jeans for the invitation, I could feel number 48 pulse with an energy that none of the others in the street possessed.

The biggest giveaway, however, was that someone else was loitering outside. A tall figure, leaning against the iron railing at the foot of the steps, one knee raised as he fiddled with his footwear.

Snitch darted a glance my way and began to slow down. "Good evening, DCI Wyld," he called, faux cheerily, and paused so that I could catch him up.

And protect him from my former boss, no doubt.

"Monkton?" I arched an eyebrow as I approached.

Snitch let me pass him, then fell into step behind me. "Owwww," he moaned anxiously. Wyld had arrested Snitch for the murder of Wizard Dodo a while ago, and the two had never really seen eye to eye since.

"Liddell?" Monkton started in surprise.

"What are you doing here?" I asked.

"I could ask you the same thing," he said.

As I drew level with him, I could see he was tying his bootlace.

"I had a stone in my shoe," he told me, as though that explained everything. Clearly, it didn't.

"But I mean, what are you doing *here*?" I jabbed a finger at the front door of number 48. I'd been right about this place. Even under the dim street lighting, I could see the gleam of the black paintwork on the door, as though it had been newly decorated. The brass—on the handle, the knocker, the letter box and the small circular bell to the side of the jamb—had been freshly polished too.

"I was invited." He slipped a hand into his jacket pocket. He might have dressed up for the occasion. Smart suit and tie, clean ankle boots. But on the other hand, he tended to dress smartly anyhow. He produced an envelope with a flourish. I recognised it immediately. Exactly the same as the more crumpled version in my hand.

I flapped mine at him.

He curled his lip. "I imagined this was an exclusive

event, but"—he glanced over my shoulder at Snitch—"I'm going to assume that's not the case."

"Owww," Snitch complained, but quietly.

"Ignore him," I told Snitch, then smiled at Monkton. "Don't be such an old grouch," I scolded. "You're pleased to see me really."

"Am I?" He cocked his head and pretended to think. "No. No. Nope. Apparently not."

"Give over." I slapped his arm with the back of my hand and climbed a few of the steps. "What is this place anyway?"

"Presumably, seeing as you have an invitation, you know what it is," Monkton said. He was trying to be a smart-arse, but something in his voice alerted me to an edge there.

"You don't know either, do you?" I cried, voice triumphant. He'd been trying to bluff me.

He shrugged. "To be honest, not really." He gestured at the door with his envelope. "This turned up on my desk at about twenty past five."

"Did you see who put it there?" I asked, thinking of the old woman with the shopping trolley.

He shook his head. "No. I was in a meeting. It ran late."

"Don't they always?" I asked, thinking back to my time in the murder squad at the Ministry of Witches Police Department. I'd often lamented the fact that there were more than enough work to be getting on with, but periodically we would be hauled into an office or a conference room to listen to some bigwig bemoaning the fact that we weren't working hard enough. I was well out of that now, thank you very much.

"Did your mate get an invite too?" Monkton asked, giving Snitch the once-over again.

"Ow, no, DCI Wyld." Snitch slipped backwards, melting into the shadows. "Not me."

"Of course he didn't," I said. "I had no clue where Fletcher Gate was, so I asked him to help me." I peered up and down the road. "Come to think of it, I'm none the wiser."

From somewhere behind us I heard the quarter bell of the clock on the dome of the Ministry of Witches building on Celestial Street. The sound carried for miles. A quarter past six.

"The invite was for six," I said. "We're late."

"Only a bit," Monkton said, then conceded, "We'd better go in."

He followed me up the steps and stood next to me as I jammed my finger on the brass doorbell. I gave it a short sharp burst, then listened as the sound reverberated through the building on the other side of the closed door.

No-one came.

"Glad to see you dressed up for the occasion," Monkton said, without looking at me.

Cheeky blighter. "I've been at work all day—"

"As have I," Monkton returned smugly.

"But you wear suits anyway. I don't habitually wear tea dresses," I pointed out. "It's not a good look when you're chasing criminals around Tumble Town."

"When was the last time you chased a criminal, Liddell?" Monkton asked.

He had a point. I rarely ran *after* anyone these days,

although I had run away from a few horrors since starting up the detective agency. I lapsed into silence.

"Try the bell again," Monkton said. "Maybe they're having such a good time they didn't hear us."

"Having a good time? At a tea party?" I asked. It sounded like something my friend and business landlady Hattie Dashery might have enjoyed. Everyone else? Not so much.

Monkton snorted. "Don't tell me you don't like cake, Liddell. I'll know you're lying if you do!"

I chuckled. These days, since swearing off the booze, tea and cake were totally where it was at as far as I was concerned. That and a book and an early night, and I was a happy woman.

"I'm sure they'll have heard us," I said, thinking of the way the sound of the bell had echoed around the inside of number 48. "Maybe they're upstairs—"

I didn't get any further. Monkton leaned forward and across me and pressed his thumb on the button. It stayed there far longer than I was comfortable with.

I knocked his arm away. "That'll do!"

He smirked and resumed staring at the door, his expression expectant. In the natural order of things, when you're invited to a party and you ring the doorbell, the door is opened, you're greeted, you go inside, someone hands you a drink and a canapé and you make small talk.

But this wasn't the natural order of things.

Still no-one came. We waited in silence until Snitch piped up from somewhere behind us.

"Should I wait, DC Liddell? Or would you be able to find your own way home?"

Wrinkling my nose, I cast a sideways look at Monkton. He might be a sweetheart and walk back with me, but on the other hand he might be suddenly called away to deal with an incident somewhere.

Monkton, sensing my scrutiny, gave a half-shoulder shrug. "At this rate, we'll be going straight home anyway."

I scrutinised my invitation once more. "Do we have the right address?"

"Number 48. That's where we are, isn't it?" Monkton pushed against the door. It swung silently open.

"It wasn't even closed?" I asked.

"Apparently not," Monkton replied and, ever the gentleman, gestured that I should go first.

I stepped into the half-panelled hallway, my Dr Marten boots making a squelching sound on the pristine cream tiles beneath my feet. To my near left, a flight of similarly tiled stairs with an intricately carved wooden balustrade curled up to the first floor. The top half of the walls had been painted a deep emerald green and, lifting my gaze past the decorative dado rail, I noticed that the ceiling, high above us, had been painted cream with green swirls and fleur-de-lis. Dead ahead of me, a majestic old grandfather clock stood in pride of place to the left of a tall fireplace, and a portrait of some revered old wizard gazed down at us from his lofty position on the wall. To the right of the fireplace was a door, presumably leading through to the rear of the building, and to my immediate right, another door led to a front room or parlour or something similar overlooking Fletcher Gate.

"Marble, do you reckon?" Monkton asked, staring at the floor. His words echoed.

"I suppose so." My stomach had given a warning tremor. Something didn't seem quite right. I gazed around, trying to discern what the problem was. "Where do we go?" I indicated the door in front of us.

Monkton had tipped his head back, his eyes searching as though he could see the floors above. "Pretty quiet, isn't it?"

"It is."

Did he feel uneasy too?

He confirmed as much by reaching inside his jacket pocket and extracting his wand.

I pulled mine out of my bag.

Our eyes met. He nodded, then edged towards the door to our right. I followed him but hung back, my wand poised.

Placing his ear against the door, he listened for a long moment, then quickly turned the handle, pushed it open, and stepped sideways. No shots were fired. Nothing jumped out at us. He eased himself into the room and I followed him, one eye on the stairs, the other on the remaining door next to the fire.

"Some sort of study or library," Monkton announced. A fire, a little smaller than the one in the hall, blazed merrily in the hearth, and the walls were lined with fitted low-level cupboards beneath rows of bookshelves behind glass doors. The volumes contained therein appeared old and valuable and well cared for. Dodo would love it here.

Monkton jerked his chin in the direction of the hallway and I retraced my steps. If anybody had been disturbed by our entry into the library, they hadn't made themselves known.

Monkton scanned the stairs. I knew exactly what he was thinking. He'd be weighing up his options. Where would danger be most likely to come from?

"We might be overreacting," I said, keeping my voice low, but I didn't believe that to be the case, and from his pensive expression, he didn't either.

"Try the other door," he ordered, probably forgetting that I wasn't a part of his team anymore and he couldn't tell me what to do. Not that I minded. My heart was thumping a little harder, adrenaline humming around my veins. We needed to work as a team.

"I'm going to open it and everyone will jump up and yell 'surprise!'" I hissed. "It's not your birthday, is it?"

He shook his head. "Not till January. Yours?"

"September."

I placed my hand softly on the doorknob, cast one more quick look at the stairs, then twisted. Pushing the door, I stepped away, my wand raised.

Unlike the front door and the door into the library, this one creaked. It took an interminable age to fully open, but when it did, a waft of warm air rushed out at us. I recoiled. The air had an odd fragrance ...

That quickly dissipated.

I stepped inside, wand raised, drinking in all I could see. Yet another fire blazed here, burning red and orange, gleeful in the massive stone fireplace that wouldn't have looked out of place in a countryside manor. The flames flickered, reflecting on the water glasses and three or four crystal vases of flowers that decorated the sizable round table set on a rug in the centre of the room.

Everywhere there was warmth and colour. The walls

were painted in a powdery mustard with red vine decorations, the half a dozen life-size portraits on the walls depicted witches and wizards from the past, all with bright eyes and rugged colour in their cheeks. Mirrors reflected the light from the chandelier, which itself was a chaotic structure of coloured glass and small white candles. Half a dozen or so flowery teapots had been arranged on the table—the tablecloth classically white, of course—and matching cups, saucers and side plates had also been neatly laid out, with peach linen napkins and tiny ornate finger bowls. Triple-tier plate stands displayed slices of cake, cupcakes, scones, biscuits and sandwiches. There were bowls of clotted cream and mini jars of jam, jugs of milk and tiny containers of sugar cubes. It all looked fresh and appetising. The aroma of baked sugar and cinnamon and the fresh tang of strawberries fragranced the air in place of the initial musty metallic tang.

In addition to the portraits, the room had been furnished with clocks. Antiques. Some of them must have been worth a fair few bob. There were two grandfather clocks in the room—both of them taller than the one in the hall—and two slighter and prettier 'grandmother' clocks. In addition to these, there were eight elaborate wall clocks in brass and gold and silver, shining as bright as the day they'd been purchased.

Only four of them were working.

The rest had all stopped at virtually the same time. There were slight differences ... but only in the positioning of the second hands.

But even that wasn't the most bizarre element of what I was seeing.

Not even close.

I held my breath, taking in the scene, observing as steam drifted out of the spout of the teapot nearest to me. Funny how your brain concentrates on the minutest of details in times of trauma.

"Looks like we found the party," Monkton said, his morbid attempt at humour.

Because the other guests hadn't waited for us to arrive.

They'd gone ahead and died without us.

CHAPTER 3

Monkton exhaled. An audible sigh. Something complicated. A release of tension after a sudden shock? A realisation that he was the first officer on the scene? Dismay at the sheer awfulness of the sight in front of us?

Eight corpses slumped in their seats. Five of those had faceplanted the table. The remaining three were crumpled in their elaborately carved high-back chairs like half-empty sacks of potatoes. The ninth victim had slipped from his chair and fallen onto the rug.

I gaped at the figures still in their seats. Thrones for dead people.

Taking a tentative step inside the room, I scanned for hidden dangers. I spied the door at the end of the room. It was closed. Other than that, there were no cupboards, no cubbyholes, no dark corners, no screens. Nowhere that anyone could be hidden. This was a magnificent setting for mass murder, but the murderer had already made their escape.

"What happened here?" I whispered, horror-stricken by the sight of so many bodies. I'd dealt with dozens, possibly hundreds, of murders in my career, but I'd never come across a scene of human devastation on this scale. It was a purely rhetorical question, of course. Monkton could have had no more idea than me.

He was already on his phone. "Multiple homicide," he was relaying. "Nine. Yes. Get every available officer down here. Now!" The person on the other end squeaked a reply. "And alert O'Mahoney. I need him pronto."

I moved further into the room, edging around the rug, scanning the floorboards, careful of where I was placing my size eights. Pulling out my mobile, I hurriedly thumbed the camera app. If I asked Monkton's permission, he'd refuse it, so I cut out the middle man and began to film a video, slowly swivelling in place to catch the partygoers in situ, as well as all the detail on the table and the clocks and portraits on the wall.

"Help's on the way," Monkton said, and began to take his own photos. If he noticed what I was doing, he didn't say anything.

"The table was set for thirteen," I said, counting the settings, with the name cards heading every place.

Monkton huffed. "Oh, please. That's so predictable."

"But you and I hadn't arrived, and there are only nine bodies."

"So someone else was as tardy as us." Monkton fished a couple of pairs of latex gloves out of his trouser pocket and handed one set to me. "Lucky them."

Pulling the gloves on, I took a closer look at the name settings. As with the invitations, no expense had been spared. These had been handwritten on heavy-duty card. "I'd have been sitting here ..." I reached for the card to check for a watermark. The writing was the familiar looping script from the envelope. As I examined it, the ink began to fade, my name disappearing from view. I hurried to replace the card on the table but too late—my name had gone.

"Weird." Stepping sideways, I examined the card of the witch or wizard who would have been sitting next to me. Their card was blank too.

"Do you recognise anyone?" I asked, creeping a little closer to the table.

Monkton scrutinised the faces we could see. He didn't reach out to touch the corpses of those he couldn't. "Difficult to say," he said, but his gaze loitered on one grey-haired chap with lips tinged a soft blue.

"It's a remarkably clean scene," I said. "No blood. No signs of violence."

"Poison?" Monkton articulated the obvious.

"But no vomit and no frothing at the mouth." I crouched next to the gentleman nearest to me, his head turned to the side. "That's what we'd expect to see, right?"

"Owwww!" Snitch stood at the door, his hands clasped to his mouth.

Monkton jumped up, rushing over to shepherd Snitch away. "Out!"

"You shouldn't be in here, Snitch," I called over.

"But DC Liddell—"

"Wait for us outside," I said.

"But—"

"Snitch." I widened my eyes and flicked them towards Monkton.

He took the hint. "Owww. Alright." He disappeared from view, his soft tread pitter-pattering on the marble tiles.

Satisfied Monkton and I were alone again, I leaned closer to the body next to me. A wizard in his seventies, I guessed, his face worn, but his deep blue robes were expensive, trimmed with gold thread and—

He groaned, his eyelids flickering.

I shot backwards and tumbled to the floor. "Creepers! Monkton! We've got a live one!" I clambered upright and reached for the wizard, pulling him from his chair and easing him onto the rug. His eyelids fluttered.

Monkton joined me and lay his head against the old man's chest. "He's alive, but barely."

"Come on, old-timer," I crooned, pushing his forehead back, lifting his chin and making sure his airway was clear. "Help's coming!"

"Let's hope it gets here quickly!" Monkton said and jumped back on his phone.

"You're sure everyone else is dead?" Monkton's face had turned a delicate shade of green. He wasn't good around dead bodies, which, when you consider his career choice, was a tad odd. The paramedics had tended to the wizard we'd found alive—and I have to confess I was kicking myself for not checking from the get-go—and he'd been taken away in a poorly but stable condition.

I crossed my fingers, praying not just that he would survive, but, being the mercenary ex-police detective that I was, that he'd recover quickly and be able to give us a good account of what had happened here this evening.

"They're all as dead as doornails," Mickey announced. An Irishman, the official pathologist for the Ministry of Witches was definitely the most cheerful person in the room. Perhaps he liked to be busy. I hoped so, because he had his work cut out with this lot.

"You have double-checked, have you?" Monkton asked.

Mickey grinned. "I have, DCI Wyld. And so has Ruby." Mickey's assistant, a flame-haired petite foil to Mickey's exuberance, smiled and nodded while she carried on taking samples, or whatever it was she was doing with her test tubes, swabs and little plastic bags.

"I don't suppose—" Monkton began, and Mickey held his hand up.

"I know exactly what you're going to ask, and the answer, as it always is, is no. I can't tell you what the cause of death is yet."

"Ever optimistic." I smirked at Monkton.

"One of these days he'll tell me something useful in a timely fashion," Monkton assured me.

"You can live in hope," Mickey replied and, donning his mask, returned to the task in hand.

The scenes of crime photographer was busy taking candid snaps of the unfortunate corpses. Periodically, we all had to move to allow him to do his job. There were two other technicians here from the forensic team, but apart from them, Monkton had insisted that no-one else encroach on the scene. While the pathologists did their work, it gave Monkton and me ample time to survey the room and take in the finer details.

"Why were you late?" Monkton asked, his gaze roaming over the table.

"I didn't get the invitation until about ten to six," I told him. "Even if I had known the way here, I'd never have made it for six."

"Hmm." He lapsed into silence.

"Who are The Extraordinary High Society for the Endowment of Judicial Awards?" I asked.

Monkton fidgeted. "What makes you think I know?"

"You decided to turn up here," I pointed out. "Am I wrong to assume that you understood what the invite was for? Because if you did, you must know who these poor folk are … otherwise why would you cut short your working day to come here?"

"You came along too," Monkton pointed out.

"But I'm a social being," I told him. This was less true than it had been. Of late, staying in had become the new going out. "I'd go to the opening of an envelope." *And I'm a curious creature by nature.*

"I got it wrong," Monkton said, avoiding my eye. "I thought they were someone else."

"*You* got something wrong?" Puzzled, I regarded him suspiciously. "Unheard of. Who did you think they were?"

"There's a similar-sounding organisation. The *Esteemed* High Society for the Endowment of Judicial Awards."

I was none the wiser. "And what do they do?"

"I don't know how you'd describe them, really," Monkton said, musing over his choice of words. "Not Freemasons exactly, but something not too far removed."

I waited expectantly. He didn't go on.

"Is it a secret?" I asked.

"Kind of," he said, then, "Yes." He avoided my questioning stare.

I pressed on. "Is that it?"

"Pretty much."

How exasperating! My ire began to rise. "Monkton!"

Mickey raised his eyes in our direction. I smiled at him. "The boss is being difficult," I told him. Not that Wyld was my boss anymore, but the pathologist knew us from old.

"Makes a change," Mickey said and returned to the job in hand, sticking thermometers where they had no right to be under normal circumstances.

"If I google The Esteemed High Society for the Endowment of Judicial Awards, what will I find out?" I challenged Monkton.

He sighed. "Not much."

"You do realise that had I not been late, it would have been me faceplanting into my cheese and tomato quiche, do you?"

"Don't." Monkton grimaced. "I'm not sure I'll ever enjoy a slice of quiche again."

That might severely limit Monkton's options at picnics and buffets, given that he was already a vegetarian.

"You'll just have to settle for crisps," I muttered.

"Pardon?" Monkton, no mind reader, obviously hadn't been following my train of thought.

I faced him properly, raising my eyebrows. "I only want to know who it was who wanted me dead," I told him. "Who wanted *us* dead."

He swallowed; glanced around. I spotted a flicker of anxiety. That was the moment I realised something dark was at work here. Darker than mere murder. If Monkton was worried about being overheard, in a room full of fully vetted professionals, then we were in murky territory.

He lowered his voice. I had to lean in to hear him. "I can't be sure, because I don't recognise everyone at the table … but that gentleman there—" He pointed out a wizard slumped in his seat. "I reckon that's Wizard Tuttlewhirl—Tobias—I worked with him when I was coming up through uniform."

"Tobias Tuttlewhirl," I repeated, scanning the wizard with a large belly and at least half a dozen chins, the number of which was exacerbated by his final resting position. May the goddess spare me from being found in such a way. Not that it mattered in the grand scheme of things …

I inched a little closer, running the risk of being on the receiving end of Mickey's furious glare. Tobias had donned special robes for the occasion. They were a bright yellow with saffron edging, and a band of multiple shades of blue with gold thread around the cuffs, hem, neck and edge of the hood. If you knew how to read robes, you would be able to tell which coven Tobias had belonged to and which organisations, simply by the colours used and the placement of those colours in the strips of decoration. They were rather like the medals that mundane soldiers wore.

Unfortunately, while I knew plenty of covens and could recognise their dress codes, everything else was simply hieroglyphics.

I frowned. "Yes, now that you mention it, I do recognise him." But only vaguely. Monkton and I had joined the Ministry of Witches Police Department a few years apart, but I'd still been in uniform while he was carving a name for himself in the homicide division. Tuttlewhirl had retired by then, although his name had been legendary. They'd rolled him out on one or two official occasions for ceremonies and the like. Other than that, I'd had little to do with him.

I crouched next to Tuttlewhirl and examined his face. He didn't appear to be sleeping; his eyes were slightly open, but his face wasn't contorted. He hadn't died in pain.

That was a blessing.

"You think he was the member of some highfaluting organisation?" I asked, thoughts whirling through my mind.

Monkton crouched beside me so that he could better whisper in my ear. "Could be a gathering of some well-known investigators." He shook his head. "But it's a big jump given we don't know the names of anyone else."

Remembering the placeholders, I jumped up. There had been nine people in the room when Monkton and I had arrived. The table had been set for thirteen. Thirteen minus Monkton and myself? Eleven. That meant two people hadn't shown up.

I located the placeholder with Monkton's name on it. Still visible.

"Monkton," I said. "Can you pick that up?"

"I don't want to disturb any evidence, Liddell," he reminded me.

Impatiently, I turned to the photographer. "Have you taken photos of the table?" I asked. "Specifically, the way it's been set?"

"I have—" he started.

"Could you take a detailed image of every setting—as best you can—while we still have the victims in place?" I asked.

"Of course." He began to raise his camera.

"Start with this one, please," I instructed him, then hovered over his shoulder, observing the images the photographer snapped on his digital display. "Perfect, thanks."

As he moved on to the next setting, I nodded at Monkton. "There you are. Pick up the name card."

Monkton stared at me.

"Go on!"

But as he went for it, a thought occurred to me. "No. Wait!" I reached for it instead. "Let me."

We were still wearing gloves, of course, but that hadn't made a difference before. I plucked the card up and waited, staring intently at the lettering. *DCI Monkton Wyld* in brilliant sapphire blue.

Nothing changed.

"You take it," I told him, setting it down on the pristine tablecloth.

"Why?" he asked but reached for it anyway, gripping it gently between his short fingernails. As he lifted it to get a better look, the lettering that made up his name and title rapidly faded from view.

"What's that about then?" he asked, flipping the card over. It was blank on the reverse.

"That happened when I picked up mine," I said. "Interesting that when I held yours, it didn't react at all."

"A kind of roll call?" Monkton theorised.

"Precisely."

"We should get the name cards over to the forensics lab and see what they can uncover. If there are no other identifying documents on the attendees—credit cards, invitations, whatever—the cards would help us."

"Better than that—" I slipped around the table, scrutinising each name card in turn. Everywhere that someone was sitting, the cards were blank. I was more interested in the two attendees who'd been a no-show.

"Look," I said, pointing at the first empty space.

Monkton joined me. "The card is blank." He sniffed. "That puts paid to your little theory, Elise."

"Does it, though?" I examined the setting. Identical to those others which hadn't been disturbed, except for the minutest details. The dessert fork had been knocked. The water glass had been moved.

It might mean nothing.

But it might mean that someone had sat here, however briefly.

"What about the other empty place?" I moved around. This one, with its back angled towards the corner, would have remained largely in shadow. I leaned over to take a better look at the card.

The beautiful script swirled across the creamy board.

I caught my breath. It couldn't be. "Superintendent Culpeper?" I read, peering over at Monkton.

"Culpeper?" he repeated. "The Dark Squad's Culpeper?"

"Do you know another?" I asked.

Monkton closed his eyes. "Hell's bells."

"I too can hear them ringing," I agreed.

CHAPTER 4

"He was invited, too?" Monkton surveyed the bodies, slumped in eternal repose. "Tuttlewhirl. Me. You. Culpeper. That's a definite theme."

"Not one I'm keen on," I admitted. "And who are these other people?"

"I have something interesting here," Ruby called. She'd been tending to the only woman at the table. The corpse's witch's hat had been knocked to the floor as she slumped forwards, revealing a short-clipped silver haircut, one that had recently been buzzed in around the edges. She pulled up the woman's right sleeve, exposing the inside of her arm, up near the elbow fold. There was the faintest of tattoo outlines on the skin.

Monkton and I slid closer to her to get a better look, treading delicately as we did so. Mickey joined us as well, pulling a magnifying glass from his pocket.

"It's too faint to make out what it is," Ruby ventured, but Mickey, after taking his time studying the edges of what he could see—the slightest blush of ink—flashed me a glance. I frowned back at him, but he clamped his lips together and I knew it was pointless to ask him anything.

Ruby raised her eyebrows. "What's even more interesting is this lady has some skin slippage."

"Ugh!" Monkton gagged and shot backwards, colliding with one of the other technicians who'd also been trying to sneak a peek at what we were all looking at.

"Where?" Mickey asked, and Ruby dropped to her knees on the rug and pulled the left sleeve of the woman's dull burgundy robe up past the wrist.

"See there?" She indicated a spot somewhere between the hand and the wrist. I couldn't see anything of interest at all, but Mickey nodded in appreciation.

"Good catch!" he said.

"What does that mean?" I asked. "Skin slippage?" Monkton was studying one of the grandfather clocks with assiduous interest, so I guessed asking for the gory details was down to me. "Isn't that something you see when a body's been in the water?" That's the only time I'd come across it. I'd seen more than my fair share of bodies rescued from the Thames.

"That is *one* of the reasons why you see skin slippage," Mickey agreed. "Another one"—he met Ruby's eyes and she nodded—"would be cosmetic alchemy."

"Cosmetic alchemy," I repeated in wonder. I'd been the recipient of this once upon a time and hadn't found it much fun.

"Cosmetic alchemy is a temporary alteration of the skin's cells," Mickey recited. "Depending on the skill of the cosmetic alchemist—and there are some notoriously dodgy ones around—the cells that form tissue and muscles and even bone can be subjected to a magickal force to completely alter the way someone looks."

"I know that much," I said, but not impatiently. I'd put away a few shysters in my time—back street alchemists who claimed to be licensed for cosmetic beauty but had caused untold damage and suffering to their clients. The profession attracted weak warlocks and low-level witches and wizards.

"The point is, cosmetic alchemy will always only be temporary. Any good cosmetic alchemist will ensure that the client is fully appraised of how to undo what has been done."

"In a bath bomb form?" I asked.

"Or a shower melt, or sometimes a lotion or something similar. But bath bombs are generally the biz."

"Right." I peered more closely at the anonymous female corpse's wrist. Now that I knew what I was looking for, I could definitely see some wrinkled skin around the top of her hand.

"Of course, if you're happy with the way you look, you can just let the spell run its course. Eventually you'll notice that your body is changing, and that's your cue to visit your cosmetic alchemist of choice and have the spell renewed."

I stood up and stretched, thinking. "Are you suggesting …"

"I'm not suggesting anything," Mickey chipped in quickly. The goddess forbid he speculated on something. I completely understood why Monkton found him annoying at times.

I decided to ask a blunter question. "Do people permanently alter their appearance with cosmetic alchemy?"

"They can't," Mickey reminded me. "All things come to pass. Nature will always win. That's the way the universe works."

"Cosmetic surgery can make permanent changes," I pointed out.

"Surgery, despite the fact that it's come a long way over the past couple of hundred years, doesn't work with nature, only against it. Magick will always work *with* nature."

"Sometimes for good," Ruby said.

Mickey nodded. "There's no denying that."

"So can I at least take from this that this woman—assuming she's a woman—"

Mickey grinned in devilment. "That's a whole other level of cosmetic alchemy—"

Monkton groaned. He might not have been looking at us, but he was listening.

"She was trying to alter her appearance for a protracted period?" I finally spat my question out. "Maybe not permanently, but long term—"

"Elise, my friend." Mickey cut his eyes at me. "You know there's no way I can definitely answer yes to that question. I can't get inside her brain and find out what her motivation for having cosmetic alchemy was."

"What reasons are there?" Ruby asked. "To make yourself younger or more attractive?"

"As a disguise," I said, thinking back to when Superintendent Culpeper had persuaded me to use the services of Wizard Filigree, the Dark Squad's own cosmetic alchemist.

Monkton, still refusing to look at the body, cleared his throat. "Or to hide in plain sight," he added.

———

Sometime after three in the morning, the final body was transported away, leaving Monkton and me alone with the room. Several members of his team were posted outside in the street, and a couple of others were searching the rest of the building.

I had taken the opportunity to nip around myself a little earlier, while Mickey's team were attempting to move the corpses, leaving a less than enthusiastic Monkton to oversee the operation. And what an operation it had been. Given most of the alleys and lanes in Tumble Town were far too narrow for cars, Tumble Town hearses tended to consist of single mules pulling a long, flat bier on wheels. The procession of these hearses would have made for solemn viewing. I had no doubt at all that word of this tragic tea party would be all around town by morning.

I'd headed upstairs and been astonished to discover that not only was the rest of the building entirely uninhabited, but parts of it—namely the kitchen at the rear on the ground floor, and the two rooms and the bathroom on the uppermost floor—were also uninhabitable. The rain had come through holes in the roof, the plaster had crumbled and the wallpaper peeled away. Those furnishings that had been abandoned here had rotted or were covered in mould, and most of the fittings in the kitchen had been removed. Or stolen. One of the two.

I couldn't quite get my head around it. The hallway and

the library and dining room were immaculate, beautifully original, the furnishings exquisite and chosen with great care. And nothing in these rooms could have been described as new. That was the other odd thing. The wallpaper was weathered by decades of smoke from the fires that burned in each of those spaces. The tiles around the grates were worn and chipped in some areas, but clean. The grates had been blacked and polished to perfection, and yet they were clearly old. Originals, even.

This had been confirmed when I returned to the murder room—as I'd started thinking of it. Monkton had taken down one of the portraits. The one above the fire. It portrayed a distinguished—although by no means elderly— witch in midnight blue robes with a silver thread that matched her silvery hair. She clutched a book to her chest and held an orb in the other hand. Once removed, we could plainly see the outline on the wallpaper where she'd hung for many, many years.

"Are we supposed to imagine that only three rooms are utilised in this whole building?" I asked Monkton as he pressed his hand against the wall where the portrait had been. A standard manoeuvre. He was checking for secret rooms or hints of magick that might unlock some covert passageway.

"I guess so." Monkton removed his palm and turned around slowly. "Did you notice that only four of the clocks are working?"

I resisted the urge to thump him. *Well, yes, obviously I did, Monkton. I didn't earn my MOWPD badge by performing romantic favours for my superiors.* But least said, soonest mended. He was my ex-boss, after all. I smiled sweetly. He'd permitted me to stay here even though I was no longer a member of his team. That had been generous of him.

Unless he'd forgotten. Old age and decrepitude and all that. Some of his current team's newer members had given me sly eyes, undoubtedly wondering why I was here at all, let alone working with their guvnor, but I ignored them. I was too long in the tooth for drama.

"I did notice that," I said. "And, those eight all stopped working at around quarter past six."

He grunted. Perhaps he'd imagined he'd got one up on me.

"I've taken a video. I'll have Wootton take a look and see if there's any significance about the time at all, but it seems as though they all stopped working when the victims died." Monkton crooked an eyebrow. I knew what that meant. This is *my* case, not yours. "Don't worry! Of course, I will cc you into any of our findings!" I hurriedly added.

Monkton huffed. "I'm sure my team are completely capable of carrying out this investigation, Liddell."

Uh-oh. He'd finally remembered who had proper jurisdiction here and who didn't. I'd need to keep him sweet.

"I know that," I reassured him. "But I figure with eight corpses, you'll need everyone on board tracking down who they are and what they were doing here. I want to do my bit, however small." I tried to make myself sound humble, bowing in deference to his superiority, but I'm not sure I did a particularly good job.

I took a final look around the room. The forensic team had been over everything with ultraviolet light and magnifying lenses and had fingerprinted every inch. The food and drink had been photographed and carefully taken away in containers. Every glass, cup and saucer, teapot and item of cutlery had been catalogued and bagged. Even the peach linen napkins were en route to the MOWPD's dank underground laboratories, where such things were processed and stored.

So thorough had Monkton's team been, I had a feeling that if I didn't keep moving, I'd be likely to find myself with a tag around a finger and a number stencilled on my forehead, lying prone on a bier and enduring an uncomfortable, bumpy ride back to Celestial Street.

"It's getting late," Monkton said. "We should come back and look at it with fresh eyes tomorrow."

I stifled a yawn. "It is tomorrow." He was right. If we carried on we'd be liable to miss something. I'd probably only managed a few hours' sleep in the past twenty-four. My brain wasn't firing on all cylinders, and I was certain that I'd overlooked something. I had a nagging feeling in the back of my mind that there had been something I needed to pursue.

But like steam, the thought had dissipated into nothing.

I followed him out into the spacious hallway. Without anyone tending to it, the fire had died down hours before, and now one of the forensic investigators was combing through the ash and coals with a pair of long tongs. I doubted she'd find anything in there relating to a poisoning, but I suppose she had to try.

Monkton was checking in with the uniformed officer stationed at the door. This one held a clipboard and signed people in and out of the crime scene. While I waited for

Monkton to finish up, I glanced over at the library door. It stood ajar.

I wandered over and peeked inside, expecting to see a member of Monkton's team, but the room was empty.

And the fire still burned.

I frowned and stepped inside. Who'd been feeding the fire? And why would they do that when the grate would need to be searched sooner rather than later? I regarded it with interest. No coal scuttle. No wood basket. No fireside companion. Not even a poker.

I retraced my steps to the murder room. There were none of those items in here either. And that would explain why the fire had gone out. It was the same story in the hallway.

"I don't suppose you have a pair of gloves I could steal from you, do you?" I asked the woman on her knees with the tongs.

"Of course!" She rummaged in the toolbox all forensic personnel seem to be married to and presented me with a fresh pair.

"Thanks." Pulling them on, I returned to the library.

I tugged open the cupboards in turn, but, without exception, every single one was bare. They had that old empty cupboard fragrance too, one that reminded me of my grandparents' house years ago, after my grandpa had died and my grandmother had cleared all his things out.

The dusky scent of fading memories.

Carefully closing the last of the doors, I crouched on my haunches in front of the fire and pulled the latex gloves free of my fingers. That wall of warmth after a long, busy day—couple of days—instantly had a soporific effect. I rocked a little as I watched the flames. They danced with enthusiasm, not ready to dampen down any time soon.

"Magick," I whispered, because when all other possibilities are exhausted, what else can it be? I yawned and rolled my head around my shoulders, hearing the satisfying cricks and cracks of my vertebrae, then tilted my face upwards. Time to go. If I didn't make a move, I'd fall asleep right here.

A shadow passed in front of the mirror, and I stood, thinking this must be Monkton's reflection. He'd come to find me?

But the room was empty. He hadn't. No-one had.

Moving to the doorway, I peered out into the hall. Monkton was talking into his mobile while rubbing his eyes. The uniformed officer on the door shifted his weight from one foot to the other. The forensic technician was sweeping ash from the hallway's fireplace into an evidence bag.

I returned to the centre of the library.

"I'm shattered," I said aloud, stepping closer to the mirror. Chances were I hadn't seen anything at all. It was a trick of my tired eyes, or the flickering of the lights. The electricity supply into Tumble Town was dodgy at the best of times. Many houses and all of the street lights and lamps still ran on gas.

But, as I paused there, my pale face reflecting back at me, dark circles beneath my eyes, my multicoloured hair an unkempt mess, I had a sense of something staring right back at me.

A shiver ran down my spine, the hairs on the back of my neck prickling. I inched closer to the mirror, the fire warming my legs. Reaching out, I ran my index finger down the glass, leaving a greasy smudge. As solid as you'd expect it to be. My skin didn't react at all; no tingling. No sense that there was some energy field here.

"Do you want me to walk you home?"

I jumped. Monkton was at the door, ready to call it a night.

"We'll walk together," I told him without looking round. "We're both going in the same direction." Hopefully one of us would find our way.

"Rightio." His phone started to ring again. "Give a man a break," he grumbled. "Wyld!" He barked his traditionally terse greeting and I smiled.

My reflection smiled back at me.

Nothing to see. Just me.

It wouldn't surprise me if there were ghosts inhabiting this house. I'd have to get Ezra to pop over and see what he could deduce.

"Yeah," said Monkton. "No problem. I'll send someone over." He hung up and I turned away from the mirror.

"Could you have the mirror taken off the wall tomorrow?" I asked. "I'd like to get a look behind it."

"Really?" Monkton flicked his eyes at it. "That's a monster. It'll take a team to get that rotten thing taken down. I've had the house swept for portals, if that's what you're thinking."

"I don't know what I'm thinking, if I'm honest," I told him. "I'm not sure my brain's engaged at all."

"Time to head home and get warm," Monkton agreed.

"It's quite nice by the fire," I told him. "I was considering curling up right here."

His forehead creased in bemusement. "Maybe. If the fire hadn't gone out hours ago."

"No—" I turned back to point at the blaze.

Except there wasn't one. No flames. Not even a hint of embers. The grate was full of ash. Cold, grey ash.

Stumped, I stroked my thighs. My jeans were still warm from the heat.

"Let's go," I said.

CHAPTER 5

"I'll see you in the morning," Monkton called as we finally split up. He was heading to his little house on the other side of Celestial Street while I'd worm my way down a few back alleys to get where I needed to be.

Given we'd recently heard the Ministry of Witches clock chime quarter to four, morning was already upon us, but I simply waved and turned away from Cross Lane. Peachstone Market wasn't far, not as the crow flies, but I decided to keep my wits about me. Tumble Town comes alive once darkness falls, and it only really quietens down again after four. There would be strange and cunning folk about at this hour, and I wanted to make sure I made it home in one piece.

Despite being on my guard, every nerve and fibre primed and listening out for movement close by, I nearly jumped out of my skin when someone cleared their throat behind me.

"Ahem."

I spun around, my hands raised in front of my chin

defensively, prepared to practise ju-witch-su if necessary. But the hooded figure cringed away from me.

"Sorry! Sorry! Didn't mean to startle you, DC Liddell!"

"Snitch?" I asked, and if I sounded cross, it was probably because I was. I should have recognised the plaintive, strangled sound of his voice. "Have you been following me?"

"Well, yes, DC Liddell. I waited for you outside but you was wiv DCI Wyld—"

I gaped at him. "You've waited for me all that time? It's four in the morning!" The boy was a fool. I'd like to say that any sensible being would have been tucked up in their nice warm bed at this hour, but this being Tumble Town, that didn't hold true.

And besides, I could never be sure Snitch had a house, let alone a bed, although he claimed to live in the same house he'd been born in.

He was a mystery, was Snitch.

He sniffed, and I couldn't tell whether it was because he felt hurt by my reaction or whether he had a cold coming. "I wanted to make sure you got home alright."

Bless him. "That's really sweet of you, but you know I wouldn't have put you out—"

"Oh no, it's fine! I didn't have nuffin else to be doing."

We walked on, him following just behind me because the alley wasn't wide enough for the two of us. I was glad of his company, in a way, especially when we stumbled on a couple of tall figures hanging out in a courtyard. I caught a flash of metal as one of them hid his hand in his robes.

I raised my eyebrows. Patted the pocket where I kept my wand. A knife?

"Alright, Jarrow?" Snitch asked in his soft voice as we walked past them.

"Alright, Snitch?" A deep voice returned his greeting.

"Stay out of trouble, Snitch," the second man, younger, called after us, sotto voce. The three of them cackled, but softly, like well-fed crows.

Ah, there's honour among thieves, that's for sure.

"I do my best," Snitch whispered. Only I could have heard him.

We walked on in silence until finally we arrived at Peachstone Market. The square was deserted. Not even the feral dogs who roamed the lanes hereabouts showed their faces. Perhaps they were asleep beneath the empty stalls.

"Thanks, Snitch," I said as we approached the fountain. Once upon a time, a beautiful young woman had sold flowers here. I thought of her every time I passed by. There were often simple posies left here. I thought I knew who it was who left them, but I'd never seen him again.

That reminded me of Culpeper.

He'd been invited to the tea party, but he hadn't shown up.

Or had he?

"My pleasure, DC Liddell," Snitch said, and paused beside the fountain, twisting his hands.

All I wanted was to head inside my building, clump up the stairs to my flat and dive under the covers, but I could tell that Snitch was dying to offload something.

"What's up?" I asked.

"I s'pose it's somethin' and nothin' really ..."

"Spit it out, Snitch. I need to be in the office in a few

hours." Just saying those words hurt. It was hardly worth going to bed.

"Well, the thing is ... I mean ... maybe it's not important ..."

"Go on," I urged him. Honestly, I was going to have to wring his neck.

"Someone came out of that house soon after you went in."

That stopped me in my tracks. I experienced a rush of adrenaline; a sudden sense of sobriety even though I hadn't touched a drop of alcohol for months. "Someone?"

"In light grey robes."

Neither Monkton nor I had heard or seen anyone. How had he snuck past us?

"Not young, I wouldn't have thought," Snitch added, unconsciously hunching a shoulder. "But not old." I filed that away.

"Are you absolutely sure?"

He nodded, his face ghostly white in the light of the nearest lamp, eyes wide.

"You didn't think it was worth mentioning at the time?" I asked, trying to keep my voice level. But, come on! Why should he have? People go in and out of buildings all the time. That's what they're supposed to do. That's what doors are for.

"I did try," Snitch wheedled, and I recalled how he had, in fact, popped in to tell me something, and I'd promptly sent him away.

"My fault." I pinched the top of my nose. My eyes were scratchy. "I don't suppose—"

"I did follow him a little way, DC Liddell."

I perked up at this. "You did?"

"I lost him in Corbett Lane, where it meets The Burial Place up there. Bit of a rabbit warren to be fair, but I can ask around ..."

What would he be asking for, though? *Did anyone spot a stray man trotting up the lane? What did he look like, lovey? Oh, y'know. Not old. Not young. Grey robes.*

Yeah. He'd be on a hiding to nothing. But at least it was something.

"That would be fab, Snitch," I said, then pointed at my building. "I need to go and get some shut-eye. Do you mind?"

"Of course not, DC Liddell! You have a rest. I'll see you later."

Grateful, I tottered a few steps towards the communal front door. "Later, in the office?" I asked as an afterthought. "I might be back at Fletcher Gate."

"I'll find you," Snitch called softly and, gliding backwards, disappeared into the shadow of the abandoned market stalls.

Given how exhausted I was, I should have lapsed into a coma the second I threw myself down on my bed. Unfortunately, as is often the way when you're absolutely done in, I couldn't sleep properly. I dozed instead, lapsing in and out of some kind of semi-dream state. I'd been careless.

Hadn't I cottoned on to the fact that someone had been inside the murder room, handled their place name card thingie and gone again? Why hadn't I followed that up?

Perhaps more importantly, neither Monkton nor I had searched the property thoroughly enough after discovering the horror in the murder room. That had been dangerous. Either of us—or both of us—could have been killed.

Clearly the person Snitch had seen rushing from Fletcher Gate needed to be tracked down. At the very least, he would be a witness. At the worst, he could be our murderer.

But had a *single* person been responsible for all this mayhem? Eight corpses? Potentially thirteen?

And at least four of us would have been detectives or investigators.

I didn't like it one little bit. Maybe it was too early to draw conclusions, but it was a pattern that rang alarm bells.

And what about Culpeper?

Had he turned down the invitation? Not received one? Turned up late and seen the commotion and backed away? That would be his style. The Dark Squad liked to keep themselves incognito.

But that was assuming it hadn't been Culpeper who Snitch had seen dashing away from Fletcher Gate. Could he be involved somehow?

Anything was possible. I couldn't rule anyone out.

One thing was clear; I'd need to speak to Culpeper. And at my earliest opportunity.

Throwing my quilt aside in frustration, I sat up and scowled. I always slept with my bedroom window cracked open—I appreciated the circulation of air no matter what the temperature—and the curtains wide. From outside came the clopping of hooves, the clanking of scaffolding poles, the clinking of bottles and the thud of boxes as they were unloaded from wagons. The stallholders were starting their day. Lifting my chin, I inhaled. The faint salty tang of frying bacon.

The twisted little witch from The Small Fry cabin had opened for business.

My stomach rumbled. *Later*, I promised.

From the corner of my bedroom, my stinky running shoes glared at me. I glared right back. I had no energy. "You can bog off," I said, and instead dragged my sorry backside into the bathroom. A long, hot shower and a hair-wash, paired with a pot of coffee and I might, just might, make it through the rest of the day.

"Morning, boss!" Wootton breezed cheerfully.

"I know it is," I grumbled. "Is the coffee pot on?"

"It is now." Wootton slid out from his chair and made a beeline for the back office where our kitchenette was located. As he dashed past Dodo's desk, he accidentally, or perhaps not so accidentally, made contact with the edge of it. Half a dozen books that Dodo had carefully piled up there scattered across the top in front of the slumbering wizard.

Dodo awoke with a jolt. "What the devil's going on?" he roared. "Why are you having a party at this time of day?"

Silently cursing my young office manager, I soothed Dodo the best I could. "It's only half eight," I told him. "We're not having a party."

"In my day, we went to the pub and started the party

after closing time. You young people just get earlier and earlier—" he blustered.

"It's half eight *in the morning*," I told him. "And you don't need to worry. There'll be no parties today, I can promise you that." I massaged my forehead. It was a paracetamol and coffee kind of day, with a shedload of carbs. None of it would be good for me, but somehow I would make it through.

Trooper that I am.

Ezra, feet up on his desk—his habitual pose—and reading a newspaper, glanced up long enough to smirk at me. "I could have sworn you left the office on time yesterday so you could get a good night's sleep."

"I did," I told him, settling myself into my chair at the spare desk. Once upon a time, I'd hoped that the lovely Victorian desk that Dodo had died at would be mine. Unfortunately, Dodo hadn't seen fit to vacate it—neither the office nor the desk—and I'd been lumbered with his cantankerous, albeit occasionally useful presence, and a bog-standard, no-frills Ikea desk that didn't quite lend me the air of prestige I might have hoped for as the owner and originator of the Wonderland Detective Agency.

"So, why do you look as though you haven't slept for a week, and why has your phone been ringing off the hook for the past hour?"

"Has it?" I glanced at it. It was silent enough for now. "Who's been calling me?"

"I don't know. I didn't answer it."

I tutted. That was Ezra all over. He preferred to stay in his own lane, meandering through life—now death—at his own speed. In all the years I'd worked with him at the

Ministry of Witches, he'd minded his own business and done his own thing. Which was not to say that he wasn't a team player—he'd been the best partner I'd ever had—just that he preferred to pick his team. Once he had, he remained incredibly loyal to them.

And here he was, still working with me.

"I've switched it over to mine," Wootton told me as he came out of the kitchen carrying a tray. This time he was careful not to disturb Dodo, who had straightened his books and returned to dozing. Or at least his eyes were closed, his chin was slumped on his chest and his whiskers were blowing in and out in time with his non-existent breathing.

Wootton deposited the tray on my desk: the coffee pot, my mug, a milk jug and a paper bag on a plate. "I bought a croissant on my way in," he said.

"For me?" I was touched.

"It was for me, but your need appears to be greater than mine this morning, Grandma. I'll pop out and get myself another one a bit later on."

Ezra snorted.

"You're too kind," I said, but accepted the pastry in the spirit in which it was offered, winking at Wootton. He was a cheeky blighter at times, but I enjoyed his company and his work ethic and the fact that he was hungry to learn.

"Does this have anything to do with you?" Ezra asked conversationally.

I pulled my snout away from the paper bag and looked up to see him waving the front page of *The Celestine Times* at me.

Slaughter House! screamed the headline. I couldn't see

the rest of the content, but those two words pretty much told me all I needed to know.

"Probably." I placed the croissant down on the plate, my appetite somehow diminished. The office quietened. Ezra and Wootton gazed expectantly at me, hopeful of a decent anecdote. Dodo was quiet, but I guaranteed he'd be listening in.

"On my way home last night, I had a mysterious encounter." As I said the words I found myself capitalising them. A Mysterious Encounter. Elise Liddell's Mysterious Encounter. Top Private Investigator Elise Liddell's Mysterious Encounter.

That was a measure of how tired I was.

"I received an invitation to a tea party," I told them. "And when I turned up, DCI Wyld was there. He'd been invited too."

Ezra twerked an eyebrow. "Where was my invite?"

"You're already dead, Ez," I reminded him. "There was little point in inviting you."

"Ooh." He sat straighter. "What are you saying?"

"I'll get to that." I poured my coffee, opting to take it black this morning. "No-one answered the door, so we went in and found"—I almost laughed in disbelief at the memory of it—"nine bodies around the table."

Ezra whistled. "The paper says eight."

"That's probably because their reporter arrived after the only survivor was taken to hospital." I glanced at my computer. I hadn't even turned it on yet. I did so now. Perhaps that's what the phone calls had been about. Someone letting me know that the survivor was now an ex-survivor. I hoped not. I wanted answers.

Via Monkton, of course.

"The table was set for thirteen. DCI Wyld and I should have been there."

"Thank goodness you weren't!" Wootton sounded properly horrified, his hands clasped just below his throat. "Was it poison?"

"That seems like the most logical assumption," I admitted. "But I haven't heard anything definitive yet." I typed my password in and waited for the home screen to light up, eager to catch up on my emails.

"Soooooooo?" Ezra drew the word out, his furry caterpillar eyebrows wiggling in anticipation.

I knew exactly what he was asking me. "Are we involved in the investigation?"

"Are we?"

I inhaled deeply. "I don't see why not. DCI Wyld didn't appear to be averse to me being there last night, and he did say I could meet him back at the house today. And besides … it could have been me!"

"We'd definitely investigate your murder," Wootton told me, face completely serious.

"That's good to know," I told him.

"Assuming they didn't pay anyone to bump you off in the first place," Wizard Dodo muttered. "I wouldn't trust that lad as far as I could throw him."

"That's nice, that is." Wootton pouted. "I wouldn't do that. I'd be out of a job then."

I momentarily considered this. Was that the only reason he wouldn't hire someone to bump me off? I reached for my coffee again.

"What's the plan?" Ezra wanted to know.

I sat back and tried to get my thoughts straight. "I need to talk to Minsk," I said. "Or Culpeper. But I'll settle for Minsk for now." I pointed at Wootton. "Can you do a background search into Tobias Tuttlewhirl?"

Ezra almost fell off his chair. "What about Tobias?"

Oopsie. It hadn't occurred to me that Ezra would know Tobias. Of course he would. "Sorry." I grimaced. "He was one of the victims."

"Huh." Ezra grunted. "You do know he was my boss back in the day, right?"

"Oh, sorry. I forgot. Yours and Wyld's." I nodded.

"Wyld was still wet behind the ears back then." Ezra slumped back in his chair, thinking.

"Maybe you could help Wootton put together a dossier on him?" I gently suggested. I knew all too well what it was like to lose a much-loved colleague.

"Of course," Ezra agreed.

"There was something else I wanted you to do, though." I hesitated, not wanting to intrude on his grief, but when he looked back up at me, his expression was as clear and sharp as ever. "You ... and Wizard Dodo," I continued delicately, waiting for the grouchy old wizard to erupt.

But he didn't. He regarded me with fresh interest, his eyes glowing with light.

"I'd like you both to pay a visit to 48 Fletcher Gate—incognito—and scout around."

"What are we looking for?" Ezra asked.

"Other ghosts," I suggested. "Portals? On the off chance that the forensic team missed any." I nodded at Dodo. "And I really want you to take a good look at the books in the library. See if there's anything odd about them, or ... Hmm. I don't know really. Just let me know anything you find."

"Sounds right up my street." Dodo seemed pleased, at least.

"We'll get right on it," said Ezra. "You can count on us."

My thoughts returned to the library and the large mirror there. "Just be careful," I said. "We have no idea what we're dealing with here."

Chapter 6

"Come on, come on," I whispered into my phone, nodding at an old woman coming towards me. She was pushing a cat in a buggy. In return, she scowled back at me.

Mind your own business, Elise, I reminded myself.

I was marching through the lanes, trying to find my way back to Fletcher Gate. Monkton had called and told me he'd been in situ after he'd briefed his team and spoken to the chief constable about the situation. By my reckoning, that would have been about ten. Unfortunately, I'd been held up by another client, so now I was playing catch-up, chasing down the lanes as quickly as I could, my mobile clasped to my ear.

I'd been trying to get hold of Minsk all morning but she was proving elusive. Of course, I understood that she might have bigger fish to fry—if rabbits fry fish, and I'm not sure that they do—than taking a phone call from me, but we were partners. That is, we were partners in a manner of speaking. Secret partners. Partners off the books. Partners, but not in any official capacity.

I thought of Minsk as my opposite number at the Dark Squad. The same rank, the same years of experience. The main difference between us—besides me now being a private investigator of course, plus her being a white rabbit —was that she and the team she belonged to worked secretively, entirely below the radar. I'd heard rumours about the existence of the Dark Squad but, until I'd become embroiled in Dodo's murder case, I'd never known they were actually as organised and active as they were. I still didn't know that much about them, but now I understood that they formed part of the MOWPD, albeit a discrete and discreet branch.

Minsk and I had agreed a year or so ago that we would work together to find evidence about a secret organisation known as the Labyrinthians. Although I'd found the culprit for Dodo's murder, there were others at large who should have faced justice. They might not have plunged the knife— or letter opener—through his heart, but they had been instrumental in why it had happened.

Added to which, there were hundreds—nay thousands —of books and grimoires, scrapbooks and notebooks, maps and other documents at large, all stolen from Dodo's, now my, office, and never recovered. Wizard Dodo was going to spend the whole of eternity attempting to track those down.

Which would keep him out of my hair and might therefore be a good thing.

"You've reached Minsk," the voice in my ear said. "I'm running late, so leave a message."

"We're all running late," I said. "And I've left half a dozen messages. What would be nice is if you could reply to one. Soon. Please!"

I thumbed the screen while skirting a dustbin that had spilled on its side. A couple of dogs were pulling items out and searching through them with a focus that impressed me. I'd worked with coppers who were less dedicated than that.

My phone rang and my heart leapt. I jammed it to the side of my head. "Hey!" I said. "At last."

"What do you mean at last?" Mickey asked, his warm Irish accent giving me tingles. "Have you been trying to reach me?"

"Hi. No!" I laughed. "I thought you were someone else."

"I hope you're not disappointed."

"How could I be?" I hoped he could hear the smile in my voice. "I can imagine how busy you've been for the past few hours. Have you had any sleep?"

"Are you kidding me? I might have managed five minutes, standing up by the vending machine at about six this morning, but other than that, no."

"That's no fun," I agreed. "Can I do anything for you?"

"Now there's a question. You wouldn't be trying to get around me, now, would you, Elise?"

"Absolutely not," I reassured him. "Just trying to keep you on my good side. I mean, we are playing for the same team, right? So, I'm sure you'll be wanting to share any findings you have with me—"

"Kind of the same team, to be sure. But I'll share the

findings I have with DCI Wyld first, you con artist, you," Mickey scolded me. "Official channels get priority."

Rats.

"Alright." I sighed loudly enough so that there was no mistaking my disappointment. "Why are you calling me then? Did you just want a dose of my sunshiny personality?"

Mickey guffawed. "Aye, maybe it was that."

I paused at a place where two lanes met. Left or right? Right or left? Or straight ahead?

"I do have something to share with you, as it happens, but don't you be telling our Monkton I told ye, okay?"

"Okay," I promised.

"The female Jane Doe from last night?"

"Yes?"

"She had a tattoo."

My heart began to beat a little quicker. I recalled him taking an interest in that. "That's right," I said.

"I've been taking a better look at it this morning. I excised the skin and we've had it under the microscope."

"Nice," I said, although such things didn't really bother me.

"It's faded, almost to obscurity, partly because someone has tried to have it magickly removed, but also because of the cosmetic alchemy our Jane Doe had had. But we've seen this design before."

"On DC Kevin Lloyd Makepeace?" I asked. "When we were investigating the Labyrinthians?"

"That's right."

Poor Makepeace. He'd been a member of Wyld's team and fallen in with the wrong people. I'd discovered his body behind the disused factory opposite The Hat and Dashery on Tudor Lane. "Are you certain?"

"Of course not. I can never be certain of anything where people have magickly altered their bodies, but I'm as certain as I can be. I've captured some images. I'm sending them on to Wyld and I'll bung some your way."

"Cheers," I said, although I would much rather have seen the body in person. "Any idea who she is yet?"

"One thing at a time, Elise," Mickey said, and I heard his weariness. "We've a cosmetic alchemist coming in to take a look at her. We have no idea whether we can resolve her original appearance, but *if* we could get her finger-prints, that would help."

"So you might never know who she was?" I asked.

"We have DNA. Cosmetic alchemy can't alter that. If she's on a database, we'll find her."

Of course. I hadn't thought of that.

"Oh, hang on." His voice became muffled. He was talking to someone else. "Gotta go. Ruby wants me to take a look at her post."

"Alright. Thanks, Mickey!" But he'd already gone.

"Oh, there you are." Monkton, waiting on the steps of 48 Fletcher Gate, made a point of looking at his wrist. "I thought you'd lost interest."

"Hardly," I told him. "I do have other cases I'm working on, you know."

He raised an insolent eyebrow. *The cheek of him.*

"I do!" I protested. "But, to be fair, I also managed to get lost on the way here."

"Ha!"

"How do you know your way around so well?" I growled.

He tapped the side of his head. "Photographic memory."

"Really?" In all the time we'd known each other I'd never heard him mention that before, although he could play the piano without resorting to sheet music, so maybe …

"Just kidding. I had one of the constables lead me here. He's ex-Tumble Town so knows his way around."

I decided that Monkton must have enjoyed a more restful sleep than me; he seemed to be in a relatively good mood. I suppose the removal of the bodies had cheered him up. Now he could examine the crime scene without tripping over corpses. He'd find that much more preferable.

"How nice," I said. "I must get myself one of those lovely young officers."

"Good luck with that." He waited for me to sign my name at the door then led me into the hallway. We were alone.

"Are forensics finished?" I asked in surprise.

Monkton shook his head. "Not yet. I've asked for the building for thirty minutes. They're taking a break. There's a twenty-four-hour café around the corner."

"Awww," I moaned. "A sausage sandwich. I could really do with one of those right now."

Monkton turned his nose up. "Eww."

"I'm that desperate I'd even join you for a vegetarian

one," I told him. "Made of beetroot and al-fa-fa if necessary."

"Alfalfa," Monkton corrected me. "But veggie burgers are pretty grim anyway. I would argue that any true vegetarian doesn't need to eat something that looks like meat, let alone tastes like it."

"You've just never managed to get over the shenanigans at Spicy Sal's sausage factory," I told him.

He swallowed and closed his eyes. "Let's not go there."

We stood in the hallway and studied it with morning-after-the-night-before eyes. Tall ceilings. Impressive chandelier. Oak panelling. Pristine wallpaper. Neat paint job. Marble floor tiles.

"You recall my friend, Snitch?" I decided now would be a good time to break some bad news.

"Young Bartholomew?" Monkton asked. "Of course I do."

"He was waiting outside last night," I continued.

"Yes." Monkton tipped his head back and stared at the ceiling.

"He saw someone come out of the building."

There was a pause. Then, "Really?"

"Yep."

Another long pause. "Blast."

"Yep."

"Did he ...?"

"Get a good look? No. Just a figure in grey robes. Not old. Not young. Slightly hunched up." I mimicked Snitch's posture from when he'd been describing what he'd seen.

"Doesn't give us much to go on."

"I know," I commiserated.

"So where was this person hiding?" Monkton twisted around. "How did we miss them?"

"Not in the library," I said. "We went in there first."

"And surely not in the dining room," Monkton added. "Although I suppose that's feasible."

"Must have been upstairs," I agreed. "But I'm surprised we didn't hear them coming down. Those marble tiles give the game away if you're wearing anything heavier than woollen socks."

"Not necessarily the murderer," Monkton suggested, sounding reluctant.

"I agree. We know there were two people missing from the table."

"I'd like to speak to Culpeper," Monkton said.

Join the queue, I thought, then reminded myself that this was not my investigation. I just happened to be caught up in it.

We wandered through into the library. I surreptitiously glanced around, wondering whether Dodo and Ezra had arrived yet. Unless they made themselves known, I wouldn't be able to tell. I was no ghost whisperer, and I quite liked it that way.

With no obvious sign of them, I turned my attention to the fireplace. It had been swept clean and the remnants of the previous evening's blaze taken away for analysis. The mirror remained in place.

"Is anyone taking that down?" I asked.

Monkton pursed his lips. "I had a couple of techies in this morning. They tried to remove it but it's bound."

"It's *bound*?" I repeated. "What does that mean?"

"It means it's magickly bound to the wall. Created with the building."

"Hang on." My head whirled. "Created ... How ...?"

"I'm just telling you what they told me, less than thirty minutes ago. The building wasn't built. Not in the old-fashioned sense."

"With builders? Brickies. Using bricks and mortar and all that?"

"Exactly. No. It was forged from magick. By wizards."

"I didn't even know that was a thing." I jabbed in the direction of the mirror. "So that can't be taken down?"

"Not without a wrecking ball or a sledgehammer."

"Well then, it could be a portal!" I exclaimed.

"I told you, we had forensics take a good look at this one, and the one in the dining room, and there's nothing in this house to suggest that's what it is."

"Hmm." I folded my arms across my chest, not entirely satisfied.

He began to lead me out of the room.

"Monkton?" I asked his back. "Why would you use magick to create a house? What purpose does it serve?"

He turned back to me and I could see that he too found this whole scenario troubling.

"I'm told that some of these places—structures like this one—exist on ancient sites. That they've been held by covens and secret sects for millennia."

"So, if I ask Wootton to run down a history of this house using the available records ...?"

Monkton shrugged. "By all means give it a go."

"I will," I said and reached inside the pocket of my leather jacket.

Monkton glanced over the top of his phone to study the table. We'd moved into the dining room. Our footsteps sounded loud on the wooden floorboards now that the table, chairs and rug had been removed. Curiously, the clocks had all remained in situ. When I'd pointed them out to Monkton, he had sniffed. "Bound," he'd told me.

"The clocks are bound too?" I had squinted at them, surprised by that.

"Apparently so." Wearing gloves, he'd demonstrated, trying to prise one of the small wall clocks away from its place. It had stubbornly resisted all attempts to do so and, when I'd peered a little more closely, I could see that there wasn't a millimetre of air between the clock and the wall. Or whatever is smaller than a millimetre. A micro-nano-millimetre, perhaps?

Now we were examining the photos he'd taken on his phone and trying to create a timeline. This was next to impossible without knowing the results of any of the medical tests or the post-mortems.

"What do we know?" Monkton asked me.

"With any degree of certainty?" I asked, walking around the imaginary table and facing him. "Very little."

"We know we arrived at the front door at approximately six fifteen. We heard the Ministry of Witches clock."

"Agreed."

"We rang the doorbell several times, waited politely, and no-one came." I gestured around the table. "No-one came because they were all already incapacitated."

I pretended to pick up something from the table.

"Meanwhile though, before we arrived, someone—we have yet to find out who—joined the party, handled his or her place setting card and left." I shook my head.

Monkton interrupted. "Didn't you say the person Snitch saw was male?"

I thought back. I'd been tired when Snitch had relayed the information. "Did I say that? I don't recall. But okay, *he* handled his place setting."

Monkton nodded.

I continued, "What we can't know is whether the robed figure that Snitch witnessed leaving is the same person. We also don't know whether the person who left was the *killer* or whether they simply had another appointment ..."

"Or whether he took flight because he was frightened by what he was seeing," Monkton finished for me.

"But whoever he is, we need to find him. He's a crucial witness." I decided not to divulge to Monkton that Snitch was probably out there right now asking around, entirely of his own volition. That would not go down too well, and I didn't want to risk Monkton bumping me off the case.

"Agreed," Monkton said. "Carry on."

Carry on? Carry on with what? I was now completely out of evidence.

"Those who had arrived on time started without the rest of us," I said, thinking on my feet. "Does that strike you as odd?"

"It was only tea and cake, Elise," Monkton pointed out.

"And sandwiches. It's really not a very British thing to do, is it?"

"That's true," agreed Monkton. "Unless someone urges you to start."

"But that would have to be the host. Who, of the victims, considered themselves the host?" I asked. "And if they were the host and they knew what was about to happen, then why not wait for everyone to be around the table?" Urgh. All this thinking was making my head ache. I needed another coffee.

"So maybe someone hosted the event but didn't realise ..." Monkton flipped through a few of the photos on his mobile, as if that might offer up a clue as to who had been in charge.

"We should check around all the local catering companies and see if anyone provided the food and drink for the event," I suggested. "It must have been brought in from outside. That kitchen hasn't been used in decades."

"I'll get my team on that." Monkton scribbled in his notebook.

"And ask around the neighbours here," I suggested. "You won't get anywhere, but you have to look willing."

Monkton scratched his eyebrow with the tip of his pencil. "Thank you, ex-DI Liddell. I know what I'm doing."

I hid a smile. Time to let him think he was in charge again. "Anything I can do for you?" I asked innocently.

He saw right through that. "Find me a killer."

"Tell me the motive and I'll do that," I replied, full of brash confidence.

Before he could respond, his phone went off. "Wyld!" he barked. "What?" He sighed. "Really? Oh, alright then." He couldn't have sounded more reluctant, so it had to be Mickey at the morgue. "I'm with Liddell. Yeah. Yeah. Yes, she is. Alright. Be there in thirty."

I tilted my head, waiting expectantly. Monkton curled his lip and returned the phone to his pocket. "Mickey wants me at the lab."

"He must have something worth showing you."

"Sometimes I think he invites me over just so he can goad me ..."

"You could try not to make it so obvious that you hate being there," I suggested.

"Dead things gross me out."

"They don't bother me."

"That's because you're strange, Liddell." He shrugged. "Anyway, he suggested you come too, so I guess you can keep me company."

"Excellent! Can I grab some breakfast on the way?"

"Ugh." Monkton pretended to barf. "Let's just get some mints for now, shall we?"

CHAPTER 7

Leaning forward, I studied the face of the corpse on Mickey's slab. "I have to agree there's something familiar about her." I frowned and flicked a look at Monkton. He was busy studying a wallchart with pictures of mushrooms and toadstools illustrated and labelled. Isn't it funny how the most attractive of those are the deadliest?

Or perhaps he was only pretending to study it.

"Would you care to join us, DCI Wyld?" Mickey asked, and chuckled. I clamped my lips together, avoiding the pathologist's eye. It was one thing for him to laugh—this was his place of work, after all—but it would be bad form for me.

"Not really," Monkton admitted, but he shuffled over anyway, and paused a couple of feet from the table, equidistant between our female corpse and a shrouded figure on the slab behind us. All told, there were six bodies in here. Presumably each of them was one of our tea party victims, but I couldn't tell for sure because they were covered up and protected from prying eyes.

Sighing, Monkton asked, "So, what do you have for me? Cause of death?"

"Not yet. The initial results of the samples we've taken have proved inconclusive. We now have throat swabs, nasal swabs, stomach contents—"

"Groooo," Monkton moaned. "Never mind. No cause of death? So what *do* we have?"

"This is our Caucasian witch, Jane Doe TT38652, recovered from 48 Fletcher Gate at zero-three-twenty-one this morning. She's five foot seven, or one hundred and fifty-three centimetres, and of slender build. She presents as a well-nourished adult—"

"I've seen more meat on a spatchcock," I ventured.

Monkton swallowed and looked away from the body, but Mickey didn't skip a beat. "She presents as a well-nourished adult of approximately forty to forty-five years of age, but—"

Ah! Now things were getting interesting. I pricked up my ears.

"I've had a cosmetic alchemist in this afternoon, and she managed to undo some of the spell that our Jane Doe had used to disguise or enhance herself. Difficult to know which. Or why at this stage. But that's not my job anyway, it's yours." Mickey met Monkton's eye over the body.

"Indeed," Monkton agreed.

Mickey pointed at the woman's hair. "See how it's grown in?" he asked.

"That's right." I leaned over to inspect it more carefully. "She had a buzz cut at the neck." But here, her hair fell in waves. It had grown perhaps five or six inches and changed colour from a reddy-orange to a duller brown, flecked with strands of silver.

"Also, see here," Mickey instructed, directing our attention to the face. I hadn't managed to see much of that this morning, bar a fleeting glimpse as she was loaded onto the gurney and wheeled away. "We now have a Roman nose ... and the eyes are a little wider apart. They may have changed colour, although it's a bit difficult to judge given the changes the body goes through after death."

"Mmm." Monkton grunted, thoroughly uncomfortable.

"This is where I lifted the tattoo from." Mickey angled an eyebrow at me, reminding me to say nothing, then picked up the woman's arm and turned it around to expose the front of the arm. A neat square of skin had been cut away near the elbow crease.

Monkton swallowed audibly, then covered his discomfort by exclaiming a little too loudly, "Ah, yes, the tattoo. Has that helped you ID her?"

"Not on its own," Mickey admitted. "But it is of interest."

"I had a text from Suni over in forensics just before we arrived here," Monkton told him. "She says that the forensic examination of our Jane Doe's clothes suggests that her robe is from the Coven of the Silver Midnight—"

I wracked my brain. Nope. I didn't know anything about them. An obscure sect, perhaps. I mentally filed the name away. That would be another job for Wootton. And Dodo, maybe.

Monkton had carried on. "The threads in the decoration indicate she was an engineer. Quite high ranking—"

Mickey, his voice suddenly soft, broke in. "All a ruse, I'm afraid."

He had our full attention. "You know who she is?" I asked.

Nodding, Mickey told us, "The DNA results came back."

"And?" I interrupted. "Who is she?"

Mickey indicated Monkton. "Are you sure our man here won't want to sit down for this?" He was only half joking.

"Who is it?" Monkton asked, impatient to get at the truth.

"An ex-colleague of yours. Superintendent Yvonne Ibeus."

"Thanks." Monkton nodded at the constable who had gained entrance to Ibeus's house on Moonstone Avenue. "Get a locksmith over here and have the premises secured. I'll have the new keys when it's done."

"Yes, sir." The constable sheathed his wand and began cleaning up the detritus left by his forceful spell: chunks of the wooden frame and scorched paint flakes, curls of metal from the lock, and melted plastic from the door itself. I could have opened the door just as easily. Come to that, Monkton could have too, but for some reason we always relied on bobbies to do the job.

And make it official.

I stood to the side, unsure whether Monkton wanted

me to accompany him inside, but he jerked his head at me. "Coming?"

I didn't argue. I followed him into Ibeus's flash pad.

I have no idea how much a superintendent makes, but it was a darn sight more than Monkton or me. Once inside the entrance hall, I gaped into the void above my head and tried not to allow envy to get the better of me. The double-width houses on Moonstone Avenue were three-floor Georgian terraces, with two mezzanine levels and a cellar. Their size was deceptive from the outside because they stretched back a decent way. Ibeus—or a previous owner, perhaps—had remodelled the layout so that a sleek staircase wound through the centre of the building, giving easy access to each floor. At the very top of the staircase, a stained-glass dome allowed light to shine through the heart of the building.

"Wowzers," I said. "Was she married?"

"Never married. No children. There were rumours of a relationship but she was discreet. She gave her all to the force."

"And yet ..." I pivoted around, taking in the spacious hallway, the tall potted plants, the charming watercolours on the walls. Two doors led to my right. A front living room. Neat and clean. The other door closed. To the left, a dining room and stairs down to the lower floor.

"And yet, indeed." Monkton pulled on a pair of gloves.

I followed suit. "You know, my whole flat would fit in the front room," I told him.

"Is that jealousy I hear, Liddell?" Monkton asked. "Because it's most unbecoming."

"Not at all," I lied. "I have everything I need in life."

"Maybe if you'd stayed with us, you'd have risen to the dizzying heights of senior management." Monkton smirked.

"I'd have hated that—you know I would." I wondered if *he* was hankering for a promotion.

"I'd have hated that too," he said, and I knew he was referring to me being promoted over his head. I laughed.

We started with the living room, not touching anything, just observing. Ibeus hadn't been here for months. We knew that because she'd been wanted in connection with her role in the Labyrinthians for all that time. She'd been identified as Taurus, the head of the Bulls —the Labyrinthians' henchmen who did a lot of the dirty work. She'd disappeared without trace. There was a thin but noticeable layer of dust over everything—the coffee table, the television screen, the bookshelves—and many of the plants were yellowing and in need of rescue, but the place was neat and tidy. Not a book or a magazine out of place.

The more we searched, the crankier Monkton became. I could see he was ill at ease going through the possessions of someone he had once respected.

Next to the front room, behind the closed door, was her home office. There wasn't much in the room at all. A modern L-shaped desk with a glass top that would show the slightest hint of a smear, an impressive leather swivel chair, a bookcase painted white displaying a few small photos in plain frames and a number of MOWPD manuals. No filing cabinets. No cupboards. No stray pencils and pens. Ibeus had been one hundred per cent electronic.

I loitered behind the chair. "She had a grand view of her garden," I said. The garden stretched away from the rear of the house. It wasn't massive by any means, but a good size for London. Trees at the end hid her from direct view of the house behind. A decent amount of privacy.

"Had she lived here long?" I queried.

Monkton was crouched next to the bookcase, his head on one side, scanning the police manuals. Perhaps hoping there was one called, *How to Become a Police Superintendent in the Ministry of Witches in One Easy Step.*

"A few years, I think." He sounded almost defensive. "I don't really know."

"Do you feel protective of her?" I probed.

"No!" he shot back.

"Oooooo-kay." I smiled brightly and moved to the window. "I understand, I do."

"There's nothing to understand." Monkton slammed a manual back into its place.

"She was one of ours—"

He snapped at me. "Liddell!"

"Alright." I held up my hands in surrender and began to back towards the door. "I get it. Nothing to see here."

"There's certainly nothing to see *in* here." Monkton sighed and stood up to face me. "Sorry."

I shrugged. "No probs."

"You're probably right. But I shouldn't feel that way. I didn't know her that well, and she was as crooked as the day is long. She let the force down. All of us."

"And now she's paid for it," I reminded him. "With her life."

"Are the two things connected?" Monkton shrugged. "I honestly wish I knew."

"That would at least give us a lead!" I brightened at this. "There's no denying that the tea party is looking more and more like a gathering of detectives. Maybe the Labyrinthians are targeting us."

"And rather than picking us off one by one, they decided to throw a party and invite us all?" Monkton sounded most put out. "Fiendish."

I grinned. "It's probably best if we don't take it personally."

Monkton grunted.

I changed the subject. "Does your team still have Ibeus's computer?"

"Yep. We have the one from her office at HQ, and we have the one that was installed here. We found a tablet, a Kindle and three mobile phones."

"Nothing on them?"

"Masses of data but nothing useful." He corrected himself. "Or rather, masses of data but nothing that we have found to be of use *so far*. I have a team on it. A team of two. It'll take them the rest of their lives to decode everything."

"Great," I said, but not with much enthusiasm.

"Fortunately, they're happy in their work, Elise. I send up the occasional box of brownies and that seems to keep them going."

"Vanilla custard slices work in my office," I told him. By now we were climbing the stairs to the first landing.

"You've come a long way," Monkton told me. "A couple

of years ago, I'd only have needed to bribe you with a glass of vodka."

"Blue Goblin vodka." I sighed. "Hecate's gift to hard-working witches."

"If only you'd help me find something, anything, any little clue, I'd buy you a crate."

"It wouldn't be much good to me now, would it?" I suppose I could sit and look at it, like some postmodern art installation.

"There has to be something here," Wyld grumbled. "What are we missing?"

I straightened a piece of wooden art on the wall beside me, something African and tribal. "It's probably obvious—"

Monkton's phone was ringing. "Wyld!" He listened— "Right. Okay. Yeah, let me know when you find out the others"—then slapped his phone against his forehead. "There goes that theory."

"What?" I frowned. "What's happened?"

"They've identified one of the other victims."

It had only been a matter of time. "And?"

"Does the name Wesley Warthog ring a bell?" he asked.

"No." Not that I could recall.

"Well, exactly. Not a well-known detective, is he?" Monkton couldn't have sounded grumpier. "Now we're back to square one, trying to find out what all of our victims have in common."

"All is not lost," I told him. "What did he do?"

"He sold hats on Cockington Lane."

Hats? *Oh.*

Monkton was right. It didn't sound like Mr Warthog

had much to do with being a detective. "Not police hats?" I asked, just on the off chance.

"Definitely not." Monkton jiggled his finger above his head. "You know ... the sort your mate Hattie makes."

"Top hats?" No, you didn't see many police officers wearing those. But perhaps the occasional detective ... "You don't think selling hats might have been a cover? It could be worth looking into."

Monkton regarded me doubtfully. "You're right. Everything is worth looking into, Liddell. I'll leave that in your capable hands, shall I?"

I must admit I was a little surprised. He obviously didn't think it was juicy enough if he didn't intend to put his own detectives on the case. "Do you want me to start now?" I asked, before he could change his mind.

"No time like the present," he replied. For some reason I was reminded of the clocks in the house at Fletcher Gate. And the mirror in the library. Were Ezra and Dodo there? Were they making progress?

"We're not going to find anything here," Monkton confirmed. "My officers already searched the whole house after she first disappeared. I'll have them come in and tear the place apart—we have a reasonable excuse to do so now that Ibeus is dead—but I'd wager my entire vinyl collection on there being nothing here that will help us. Not with this case, nor with the Labyrinthians."

"You still think they're unconnected," I noted.

"At this stage, how can we possibly know?" Monkton asked. "Let's keep our minds open."

"Yes, sir!" I beamed at him and headed back down the stairs.

"No need for the sarcasm," I heard him say.

Truth was, I was just thrilled to be so involved in this case. Despite the grim circumstances, I had a skip in my step because ... really? Doing this was what made my little heart happy!

Chapter 8

Wesley Warthog's Wigs and Wizard Hat Emporium, hidden in a crooked side alley, was a grand name for nothing very much. I approached it from a narrow crossroads and paused as I closed in on it to take stock. It was one of half a dozen small shops all in a row, two of which were boarded up. Of those still 'open', one was a haberdasher's, one a tobacco shop and the other sold second-hand books, specialising in small antiquarian Penguin paperbacks by the look of it. Just the thought of going in there made my nose itch. It was all I could do to stop myself from sneezing.

Warthog's Wigs and Wizard Hat Emporium, hereafter known as 'Wesley's Wigs', was housed in a squashed building dating back to the seventeenth century, I would imagine. The upper floors had been added to over the years. What originally might have been a single-storey building with a thatched roof, two at the most, was now four, with a 'new' roof—meaning nineteenth century—and an attic room—meaning a pigeon loft, judging by the activity up there—under the eaves.

The window had been repainted recently, dark blue, but again, I use the word *recent* to mean in the past five to ten years. *Recent* in comparison to its nearest neighbour, which hadn't seen a lick of paint since the sixties, I imagined. Perhaps the window had once consisted of bottle glass, but the small square panes had been replaced with plain glass and were in need of a good wash.

The window display did what was required, but only the bare minimum. There were mannequin heads arranged on three tiers of shelving. Some of them wore wigs—long, silvery affairs that a follicly challenged older wizard or witch might wear—and some of them wore hats. Conical hats with wide brims, top hats and stovepipes, a fez or two and a number of hoods. I could tell from the prices, scrawled untidily on handwritten cards, that this wasn't an upmarket destination.

Not a patch on Hattie's Hat and Dashery.

I caught the young uniformed officer stationed at the door in mid yawn. "I'm Elise Liddell," I told her, waving my PI licence.

"Hi there," she replied, her eyes lighting up. "DCI Wyld rang through and told me you were on your way. You can go right in."

"Is anyone inside?" I asked, peering through the dusty glass door into the gloom.

"DC Coultard was here, but he's gone."

"The searches are complete?" I was surprised by that.

"I don't think there's much to search," the officer replied, slightly crestfallen. That was the problem with being a relatively new uniformed officer. It meant a great deal of standing around, keeping crime scenes secure, but not a lot else at times. I'd found it unbearable. If ever I needed motivation to move up rapidly through the ranks, it had been my experiences of guarding premises.

Snoresville.

"I see. Thank you—" I squinted at her name tape.

"PC Lombardy, ma'am."

"Keep up the good work," I told her. "It's more important than you know."

"Yes, ma'am, thank you, ma'am."

"And it's Elise," I told her. "I'm a civilian now."

"Your reputation precedes you, ma—"

I wagged a finger at her.

She flushed. "What I mean to say is that I've heard great things, and I want to be just like you."

Awww. So young. So innocent. I suddenly felt about a hundred years old. She reminded me of how I'd felt when I first met Ezra. Intimidated by his experience and the tales of his doggedness.

And his pranks.

Now I understood he just liked to clear his cases up as quickly as possible so he could get on with his Sudoku puzzles.

"Just be you," I said. "That will be enough."

"You're a loss to the force, ma—Elise!"

I grinned. "And yet I'm still here." With that, I pushed the door open and stepped inside Wesley's Wigs. The room had a musty perfume. It had been shut up. Not for long, but long enough. I could smell a tang of chemicals too, the kind you'd find in cheaper stores. Stuff used in the manu-facturing process of cheap items.

Moving into the centre of the shop, I slowly pivoted, taking a good look around before pulling out my mobile and doing the same thing again while recording what I was seeing.

Rather like Betty's, the bakery I liked to frequent in Tudor Lane, where the ghost of old Betty rolled out her dough with plump, floury translucent hands, you could feel the weight of the floors above as they gradually compressed the timbers below, obeying the laws of gravity. What goes up will *always* come down. My sense of claustrophobia was exacerbated by the size of the space, a mere ten feet wide at the front, mostly taken up by the filthy window and the glass door, and stretching back about twice that distance. There was a plain door to the rear, painted the same bluey grey as the walls. Shelves had been hung on the wall, and the mannequin heads in black, white and red plastic, adorned with an array of headgear, stared at me with blank eyes and focussed expressions that would haunt my dreams for nights to come if I let them.

I zoomed in on a display of more colourful wigs, running my fingers through the strands of the one nearest to me. Not real hair. Simulated. Cheap. Plastic. When I took a closer look at the silver wigs I found much the same. One or two had been made using real hair, and some used horse hair, but for the most part Wesley hadn't supplied Tumble Town with quality products.

The same with the hats. The genuine items like those that Hattie would create were in short supply here. Almost everything had been constructed from plastic, or cardboard and fuzzy nylon. I found one tall stovepipe hat that had the appearance of being the genuine article, but when I took a closer look, I spotted some fraying around the brim, a little hardened glue on the binding and a sticker inside that told me it was 'Made in China'.

Nothing artisanal about these items.

The small counter offered nothing of interest either. There was an old electronic till that had been forced open, presumably by DC Coultard, a pile of large kraft carriers and a couple of tatty wholesale catalogues. That was it. No phone, no computer and not even the sockets to plug either of those into.

A cursory examination of the rest of the property yielded nothing. The 'stockroom', if that's what you could call it, housed a box of multicoloured Chinese wigs, a box of kraft carriers, a box of till rolls and a broom. The rear door opened onto an alley that ran parallel to Cockington Lane, which was even smaller and more crooked than its counterpart. As for the rest of the house, there wasn't a stick of furniture to be found anywhere. There were no belongings—not even a stray newspaper or sandwich wrapper—and no clue whatsoever as to Wesley's alternative address.

Nothing.

He had to have eaten and slept somewhere. But where? Unless ... Unless ...

I narrowed my eyes, turning round and round. Had this place been magickly cleansed? Had every trace of anything that had ever happened here been removed? Fingerprints? Warthog's belongings? His furniture? His books? His clothes?

Why?

Chances were I'd never find out either way.

Wesley Warthog had taken his secrets to the grave.

In memory of all the times I'd frozen my butt off while standing outside a victim's property while the 'proper' detectives attended to the important business inside, I treated Lombardy to a coffee from a little café down the road. "Don't worry," I told her. "There's so little of interest inside I doubt you'll be here much longer."

A hooded figure strolled whistling into Cockington Lane, clocked us, swivelled and whirled away without so much as a by your leave.

"Interesting," I said, catching Lombardy's eye. "Have you had a lot of that?"

She shook her head. "There hasn't been much activity at all. A couple of dogs. A few people peering down the passageway but not venturing along it." She pointed at a house a few doors up, facing us. "A woman at the window there from time to time."

I mused on this. Just what you'd expect, but ... I whipped out my card with the Wonderland Detective Agency details on it. "If you see anything that you think is a little out of the ordinary, but not suspicious enough that you want to inform your superiors—" I knew how this worked. No young PC worth their salt would want to make themselves look foolish. "It doesn't matter how small or insignificant it might be, give me a shout. You can call either of my numbers there. If I'm not picking up my mobile, someone will usually be in the office to take a message."

Lombardy took the card from me and scanned the small type. "What sort of thing?"

"Trust your instincts," I said. "Honestly. It always worked for me."

As I walked away, my mobile began to vibrate in my pocket. I fished it out. *Chocolate Orange*, the display read. Chocolate Orange was the code name I'd allocated to Minsk on the off chance anyone accessed my mobile. With Minsk being a member of the Dark Squad, I had to protect her identity. If everyone knew who she was, what she did, who she answered to or where she worked, her safety would be compromised.

"Hey!" I said, relieved that she'd finally managed to return my calls. "I've been worried about you." I hadn't realised until I said so that this was actually true. With numerous detectives dead, I was glad to know where my friends were.

"I hear you have a situation," she said, her voice quiet. I took that to mean she was in the office and didn't want to be overheard.

"We do. I need to speak to Culpeper," I told her.

"That will be difficult."

"How come?" I asked. "Can you get him a message? It's urgent."

"I need all of those," Minsk replied, her voice shrill, "by the end of the day."

"You can't talk?" I asked her.

"No. No, that's correct," she responded.

"Can you meet me?"

"I'll have to look into that for you. Goodbye."

"Minsk?"

The line had gone dead. "Oh. Okay," I said. "I'll take that as a no." I turned in the direction of Cross Lane, intending to walk back towards the agency and check in with Wootton, Ezra and Dodo, but before I'd travelled very far, my phone vibrated again.

Once.

A text.

From Chocolate Orange.

Rabbit Hole. 5 mins.

It took me eight minutes to get there.

I was further away than I thought. I chased along Packhorse Close, imagining that Minsk would have already lost patience, or been compelled to rush back to her office, but as I passed the derelict buildings at the far end of the tiny alley, past the small vacant lot given over to piles of rocks and old bricks, a shopping cart, mouldy mattresses and numerous split rubbish bags, and approached the tall graffitied wall that split Packhorse Close and prevented it from being Packhorse Way, I spotted the bright white of her fur in the shadows among the dense foliage on the scrubland.

I jammed myself into a doorway close by so that any casual observers wouldn't see us together.

"Thanks for meeting me," I said breathlessly.

"I can't stay long," she told me, her voice so quiet I could barely hear her. I crouched closer to the ground. It would help if I was on her wavelength, so to speak.

"I need to speak to Culpeper," I whispered.

"Don't we all," came the terse reply.

I frowned. "What does that mean?"

"Why do you need to speak to him?" She narrowed her eyes at me. A cross bunny. "Is it in relation to what happened last night?"

"Yes." She evidently didn't know all of the details. "What do you know about last night?" I asked her.

"Only what's been shared between branches so far. A party. Multiple homicides. Your old top boss."

"All of that is true," I confirmed. "Did you know my name was on the guest list? And DCI Wyld's."

I heard her sharp hiss. "But neither of you were there?"

"I was late," I admitted. "Wyld was held up at work. He was late too."

"In my opinion," my white rabbit friend remarked, "being late is a very good thing to be."

"On this occasion, it certainly worked in my favour."

"It did," Minsk agreed. "And thank goodness."

"The reason I need to speak to Culpeper is that his name was also on the guest list."

"Culpeper's?" Minsk sounded surprised. "We were working on the theory that everyone who attended was involved with the MOWPD murder squad."

"I thought that too, initially," I admitted. "But since then one of the names we've been given suggests otherwise. We're still working on a link. It will be easier once we know all the attendees' names."

"Did Culpeper arrive?" Minsk asked, and there was an edge to her voice.

"Not as far as we can tell. I'd like to pick his brains

about how he received his invite and why he didn't show—"

Minsk interrupted me. "I don't think that's going to be possible, Elise."

"I won't take up much of his time," I said. "If you can just get the message to him."

"You don't understand," Minsk said. "I can't get a message to him because he's disappeared."

It took a moment for that information to sink in. *Disappeared? Oh my!* "You don't think he could be ... dead, do you?"

"At the moment we have no clue about his mortal status."

"You need to find him," I said, suddenly fearful. If Culpeper hadn't been at the party but the murderer had managed to get to him anyway, where did that leave me and Monkton? I shivered, as though someone was stepping on my grave.

"We're aware of that, Elise," Minsk replied snippily.

"Of course you are," I reasoned. "I'd hate him to become another victim, especially if he isn't aware of what went on last night."

"You're treating him as a potential victim?" Minsk's voice softened.

Puzzled, I moved forward into the light, trying to catch sight of her, there among the brambles. I thought I spotted the shine of her eyes. "Yes. In the light of not having any reason why we shouldn't."

I heard her sigh. She sounded relieved.

Perturbed, I edged forward a little more. She slipped further away, backwards into the bracken.

"Careful," she whispered. "We can never know who's watching."

"Is there any reason I shouldn't consider him a potential victim?" I asked.

Now she snuck a little closer to me, her pink nose twitching. "Only that *we're* investigating him."

I exhaled, a little too loud, almost a laugh. "For what?"

"Murder."

"What?" I reeled in shock. Culpeper was an odd chap, there was no denying that, but I'd only ever heard good things about him.

Not that I'd actually heard that much about him at all, to be fair.

"Who did he kill?" I wanted to push her for details.

It was no surprise that she wasn't forthcoming. "I can't discuss the case."

Pressed back into the door's recess, I stared in her direction, thinking. We remained silent for a few seconds before I asked, "But you don't think he *did* kill someone." It wasn't a question. I could tell by how tense she was. She was having to investigate a colleague who was also her boss. She knew him well enough. Knew what he was capable of. But she didn't believe him to be a killer.

She only repeated what she had said before. "I can't discuss the case."

"Okay."

"I have to go. They'll wonder where I am."

"Thanks for meeting me," I said.

One of the long bramble stems drew back, then shot forwards as it was released, as though it had snagged on Minsk's fur. The rest of the bush shook in protest.

I waited a moment while it settled, then turned to go, mind whirling with the new information. Should I tell Monkton? What would his squad know about this situation? Not much, I'd imagine. Information was passed to the Dark Squad, but very little was ever funnelled the other way. Lost in thought, I began to slink along Packhorse Close, avoiding sloppy puddles and piles of unmentionables. This really wasn't the most salubrious of neighbourhoods.

"Elise!" A loud whisper behind me.

I turned to see Minsk crouching in a doorway, her cute rabbit face tense, her usually soft brown eyes tinged with red. "There's something else—"

"Go on." I huddled in the doorway directly opposite.

"We're obliged to investigate, and they've brought an outsider in—"

"That's standard practice," I reminded her.

"But I think ..." Her voice had almost disappeared. I strained to hear her. "I think Culpeper's being set up."

From the end of Packhorse Close, from the direction of the graffitied wall, came the rattle of a tin can, as though someone had disturbed some rubbish. Minsk's eyes widened in horror. "How much danger are we all in?" she asked and shot past me, a blur of white fur.

"Wait!" I called, but she'd gone. I moved out of my doorway and stared down the lane in the direction she'd gone, running towards danger rather than away from it.

"Brave little bunny," said an anonymous voice in my ear.

"Shut up," I snapped. That was all I needed, some

smart alec in the shadows with a loose tongue, spreading the word to a variety of undesirables.

"Oooh!" Giggles.

"Touchy, touchy!"

"Stay safe," I whispered to Minsk, not that she'd hear me.

But perhaps she did. Her voice travelled to me on a sudden light breeze. "You too."

CHAPTER 9

I climbed up to the attic of 125 Tudor Lane, where my office was housed, clutching an armful of savoury delights. Rather fortuitously, I'd passed Betty's bakery on my way back, and to say I was famished was an understatement. I therefore couldn't pass by without nipping in and availing myself of a steak and ale pie and one of their sausage rolls with the buttery, crumbly pastry.

And of course, I couldn't sit at my desk and eat pies by myself. So I'd bought enough for Wootton and Hattie, as well as Snitch on the off chance he decided to make an appearance. I had a feeling he would. He had a knack for turning up at just the right moment.

"Yoo-hoo!" I called as I mounted the top of the stairs. I'd looked in on Hattie in her shop, and she'd agreed to join us. She was just finishing what she was doing—steaming feathers—and then she'd climb up after me.

"Welcome back, boss." Wootton jumped up to take the goodies off me. "Lunch was ages ago."

"I know. We'll call this high tea."

"You people never stop eating," Dodo complained. I noticed that the stack of books on his desk was higher than ever and I was reminded of how I'd come across his body in this very room, surrounded by hundreds, perhaps thousands of volumes of books from his collection. A collection that had subsequently disappeared after the police had removed it to use as evidence.

"Chance would be a fine thing," I shot back.

"I had lunch, but I'm always up for a snackette," Wootton said. "I'll stick the kettle on."

"Perfect!" I slipped behind my desk and threw myself into my seat with a sigh.

Ezra glanced up from his computer. I took it as a good sign that he was busy. If he hadn't found anything out this morning, he'd have been relaxing with a puzzle book. "How's it going?" he asked.

I quickly filled him in. "An interesting development. One of the victims, the only female one, has been identified."

Ezra waited.

"Yvonne Ibeus," I told him, voice lowered. "We need to keep that under our hats."

He nodded.

"We didn't immediately recognise her because she'd utilised cosmetic alchemy to change her appearance. Probably hiding from the MOWPD, I assume. Monkton is searching her house—very posh—but isn't expecting to find anything. You can't say anything to anyone," I cautioned him.

"I'll take it to the grave."

"Very funny. We have a name for one of the other

victims, a Wesley Warthog." I paused. "Does that name ring a bell with you?"

Ezra shook his head. "Nope."

"No. Nor anyone else." I shrugged. "I went over to his place on Cockington Lane and had a look round his shop, but I couldn't find anything interesting. I did wonder whether it had been *cleaned*."

Ezra's eyes widened. He knew exactly what I meant. Before he could reply, Snitch butted in.

"Cor. Did you say Cockington Lane?" As I'd expected, he'd appeared out of the woodwork. "That's funny, DC Liddell, cos I've been making me own enquiries around there."

Ezra's face was a picture. "Have you now?" he asked.

"I have." Snitch sounded well satisfied with himself. I wondered how much of our conversation he'd overheard.

"It's fine." I jumped in before Ezra could question the wisdom of having a small-time petty criminal and police informant—Ezra's own informant, come to that—asking around for information about a case that wasn't *officially* ours. "I asked Snitch to follow up on the person he saw leaving the Fletcher Gate house."

"I see." Ezra sniffed, but seemed satisfied with the explanation. He'd have been only too aware that finding the escapee and potential chief suspect this late in the day was a virtual impossibility. In Tumble Town, finding a crook was like finding the proverbial needle in a haystack.

"What did you find out?" Ezra asked Snitch.

The clomping on the wooden stairs as Hattie dragged herself up them interrupted us. "Woo!" She panted as she crested the summit. "They get steeper every day, don't they?"

"I think they get steeper as you get older," Wootton volunteered, as he carried a tray piled with plates, a teapot and mugs through from the back office.

"What are you trying to say?" Hattie squeaked. "I'm not old." Given that Wootton figured I was old enough to be his grandma—and I most certainly wasn't—Hattie, who had at least twenty years on me, stood no chance.

"Insolent boy," Dodo thundered.

"No. I wasn't being rude!" Wootton rushed to defend his comment. "Isn't there a universal law that the older you are, the higher the stairs have to be? That way your heart keeps working out, and you're less likely to pop your clogs suddenly."

Four pairs of eyes stared at him: Ezra in amusement, Hattie aghast, Dodo in fury, me in wonder.

Only Snitch was nodding. "Very wise, that, Wootton. Wellbeing magick."

"What a load of baloney," I muttered.

"I read it somewhere," Wootton protested.

"On one of those dodgy web-side mc-thingummies, I'll wager," Dodo said.

"Website, Wizard Dodo," Snitch corrected him.

Hattie was perplexed. "I've never heard of wellbeing magick."

"It's a new thing," Wootton told her.

"Like avocado on toast and cafés that only serve breakfast cereals," Ezra grunted.

"What's a navacardo?" Snitch asked.

"It's a fruit," Wootton told him.

"Ewww."

"Excuse me?" I decided I needed to call order on the chaos. "Can we all please focus?"

"Focus?" Hattie asked, dropping onto one of the comfortable seats we kept for guests. "I thought I'd come up here for a cuppa."

"We can all enjoy a cup of tea and a snack, but while we do that, I'd like us to pool what we have so far—"

Hattie frowned, even more confused. "But ... but ..."

"I know you haven't been involved so far, but I'm going to want to pick your brains," I told her.

"Fair enough." She settled down and accepted the fork and a pie on a plate that Wootton offered her.

"Would you say you're familiar with most milliners and hatmakers around Tumble Town?" I asked her.

"Would I say I know every hatter in Tumble Town?" The fork in her hand paused midway to her mouth and she eyed me warily. "No."

"But you must know quite a few of them."

She wiggled her shoulders. "Maybe. I've met dozens and dozens over the years at various conferences and conventions. I probably have some awareness of others ..."

"What about a chap named Wesley Warthog?" I pressed.

She returned the fork to her plate. "Warthog ... Warthog ..." I could see the wheels of her mind whirring away.

"On Cockington Lane," I added, in an attempt to be helpful.

Snitch jumped in. "See? About that, DC Liddell?"

"Not yet, Snitch," I told him. "One thing at a time."

"Right, right, yes." Snitch, slightly disgruntled, took a

seat next to Hattie, staring at her pie. I nodded at Wootton and he hastily handed over a pie to Snitch too, thus distracting him for the time being at least.

"Cockington Lane? Yes, now that you mention it. It's not that I know anyone named Wesley Warthog, but ... mmm ... Cockington Lane does ring a bell. Not in a good way."

I perked up at this. "Do tell."

"Hmmm." Hattie thought for a moment, cutting chunks of her pie into easily managed mouthfuls. "If it's the place that I'm thinking of, it opened suddenly a couple of years ago. Nobody had previously heard of the owner, and the quality of his hats was, shall we say, poor."

"I've seen them," I told her. "For the most part, they appear to have been shipped in from abroad. Mass manufactured in factories in the Far East."

"That doesn't necessarily make them substandard," Hattie told me. "Everyone should be able to afford a hat if they want or need one. If they can't afford to pay the big bucks, they have every right to shop for something cheaper."

"These were shoddy," I said. "Rubbish quality."

"That's how I came to hear of this place. Word on the street among other hatters." She chewed on a piece of pie. After swallowing, she said, "I always like to know where to send people if they can't afford my hats, but given the feedback and the rumours ... I would never have mentioned the Cockington Lane place."

"Rumours?" I asked.

"Yes, rumours." She chewed slowly. "Sorry, I can't recall. This was a while back. Something was said ..."

"By who?" I asked. "Spread by who?"

"Oh, I don't remember." She laughed. "You know what my memory is like." She waved her fork at me. "It might come to me. Give it time."

Me being me, and being knee-deep in corpses, didn't think I had much time, but what can you do?

I smiled. "Of course. Let me know if you remember anything."

She nodded and returned to the essential business of consuming pie. "Will do."

I turned my attention to the next person on my list. "Ezra?" I tilted my head in his direction and he began.

"48 Fletcher Gate is an interesting building. I believe Wootton has some information for you about it."

"Okay." We all looked expectantly at Wootton instead.

He hurriedly scooped up a sausage roll and returned to his desk. Taking a quick bite, he scrolled through whatever was on his screen. "Oh yeah, here it is," he said, mouth full. "48 Fletcher Gate. The earliest mention of a dwelling at this address is in the parish registers of 1602." He swallowed. "Details are obviously scant, and given the issues we have searching these registers, I probably don't have the fullest information. But!" He waved his sausage roll in the air. "What I can tell you is that, so far, I haven't found a change of ownership."

"Seriously?" I asked.

"Is that unusual?" Hattie enquired.

"Unless you live in a stately home or a castle that's handed down between generations, I'd say so," Wootton answered. "But even then, there's a chain of ownership."

Ezra had a different take. "Although I have seen instances of that in the past."

Wizard Dodo, lips pressed together, nose wrinkled, nodded.

"How does that work then?" Wootton asked.

"When a property or a piece of land is owned by an organisation or institution, it can be handed down for generations."

"And centuries!" Dodo chipped in. "Many covens, many magickal sects, many cults. Families of vampires. They maintain a property in the name of the organisation or family rather than through a string of successive individuals."

"That makes sense," I said. "DCI Wyld mentioned that the property is bound and that it was magickly constructed on an ancient site."

"There you have it," Ezra said.

"Fascinating," Dodo agreed. "I had a sneaky feeling that was the case when we visited it this morning."

"Don't mention vampires," Hattie complained.

A collective shiver passed through the office.

"Ugh," said Wootton.

"But we're not talking about vampires in this case, are we?" I asked Wizard Dodo.

"No," he admitted. "You won't find many of their ilk in Tumble Town."

I allowed my brain to skirt over the definition of 'many' for now. I really didn't want to know. "DCI Wyld was correct. 48 Fletcher Gate is a building that is owned by a coven or an organisation or a group of individuals. Presumably The Extraordinary High Society for the

Endowment of Judicial Awards or however they fashion themselves."

"No." Wootton sighed. "Or at least not from what I can find out, because ... there's nothing to find out. That organisation definitely does not exist."

"And The *Esteemed* High Society for the Endowment of Judicial Awards?"

"They do, but they're entirely above board and are rumoured to have premises behind the Grand Municipal Library in Celestial Street," Wootton told me. "I couldn't find anything else out."

I rooted through my handbag for my invitation. At first it eluded me, but there it was, scrunched up between a card for my sister I'd neglected to send for her birthday eight weeks previously, and a loyalty card for Moonbucks.

I smoothed it out on the desk and handed it over to Wootton. "See this? It has a proper header. Fully embossed with gold." I glanced over at Ezra.

He shook his head. "A clever fake."

Clever indeed. It had fooled me, and Monkton, and all the other victims.

It all looked so official. And sounded official.

"We don't have an awful lot to go on, do we?" I said. "It's a dead end as far as ownership of the property goes, and the organisation doesn't exist ..."

"That in itself can be telling," Ezra reminded me.

He was right. I took a breath. "Right." I stared down, momentarily distracted by the pie on my plate. If I didn't eat it soon it would be cold. I picked up the fork and sliced into it. A little steam wafted out along with an enticing aroma of rich beef gravy and the dusky, slightly sour fragrance of ale. "Anything else?" I asked, and tucked in, hopeful he'd have something to tell me.

"The house is clean."

I hurriedly swallowed. "Is that it?"

"That's it. No ghosts. No portals—not that I'm an expert—nothing untoward, apart from being the scene of multiple homicides."

"Oh." I couldn't quite believe it. "You checked the library?"

"I did. And I didn't find anything."

"Rats."

"Nope. Didn't find any of them, either." Ezra smirked. "I've been trying to help Wootton track down a history of the house but I'm at a loss. There's no mention of anything occurring there. Nothing untoward. No weddings, deaths or christenings. No advertisements for servants in the past. Nothing."

I puffed out my cheeks. We weren't getting far.

"Which is not to say that such information hasn't been suppressed or—" Ezra nodded at Dodo. "Eradicated."

We all scrutinised Dodo. The old wizard regarded me with those dark wily eyes of his. "Is it my turn?" he asked, and when I nodded, he cleared his throat and leaned his slightly translucent form forward in his chair, tapping an equally translucent pen on the desk, over and over. "DS Izax raises a good point. It seems likely someone has removed all traces of the history of that house from official records."

I grimaced. "Is it retrievable? Or not? Where does that leave us?"

"I can look into it for you." He batted the question

away in irritation. "But I have something more pressing for you to consider."

"Go on," I said.

"You tasked me with taking a look at the books in the library," he said, "and for the most part, they were innocuous enough."

I nodded. I'd imagined that would be the case.

"What I found interesting was the *selection* of books on display," Dodo told me.

"How so?" I asked.

Dodo tapped the side of his nose. "Elementary! If I were a librarian rather than an archivist—and there really aren't that many differences between the training of the two —and I was creating a library from scratch for a magician's apprentice, or a novice, then most of the books I would *select* are the same as those in the library at 48 Fletcher Gate."

"So no advanced magick?" I asked. "Nothing out of the ordinary?"

Dodo pouted. "I'm getting to that, girlie. Just hold your horses!"

"Sorry," I said, wishing he'd speed up a bit.

"Hmpf." The disgruntled wizard bided his time, allowing his feathers to settle. I took the opportunity this afforded to hurriedly finish off my pie.

"As I say, that was to be expected, but the completeness of that collection, that bothered me." He wiggled a finger, and the tower of books on his desk began to rearrange themselves into smaller piles. "So I began to look for differences. Even the smallest of those would tell me something. Initially I couldn't find anything, but my old master—

Jethro Salazar—he taught me a spell that only the greatest archivists can use. It allows you to search *within* books using specific search terms."

I glanced over at Ezra. Was he following this because I was in danger of getting lost. Ezra's face was a study in neutrality, however. I had no idea if he understood. Or perhaps he already knew what Dodo was so riled up about.

Fortunately for me, Snitch was paying attention. "What the gobbledegook are you on about, Wizard Dodo? I ain't understood a word you've said!"

Wizard Dodo sighed in irritation. "What am I to do with you, my boy?"

"I dunno, but I'm trying me best, Wizard Dodo, I really am," Snitch lamented.

I echoed his sentiment in my own mind. *Me too*!

"It's easy enough to understand," Dodo told him, not unkindly. "You like all those computer-me-bobs, and mobility phones and whatnot. Think of it in those terms. If your computer is a library and you use goggley-jiggy-bops to search for something, it spits out a load of results at you."

"Yeah." Snitch sniffed. "Too many. Then you gotta wade through everythin' until you find somethin' useful."

Dodo's finger shot into the air. "Exactly!" he cried in triumph. "Yet with the spell that Jethro Salazar taught me, I can use intention to find what I want and make a more thorough job of it than anything Wizard Page or Wizard Brin could come up with on goggley-wobbley-doo-da."

"Who's them, then?" Snitch asked, but I spoke over him. We didn't need to get side-tracked.

"Okay," I said. "But if you don't know what you're

looking for *exactly*, how can you be precise about what you search for?"

Wizard Dodo regarded me with an element of distaste. "You can utilise your own search engine," he told me, tapping his forehead. "I have it all up here. Table of contents. Index. Bibliography. All the data I have stored over decades of searching for the forgotten and the forbidden."

"Alright." My skin began to tingle. Hadn't I seen Wizard Kephisto do something quite similar in Devon one time? "Did you find anything?"

"Not much," Dodo admitted, and my tingles dissipated as though someone had thrown cold water over hot embers. *Marvellous*. "But that in itself was interesting."

Not for me, I thought.

"I found these." He tapped the first pile of books. Four volumes. All slim paperbacks. "Plants and herbs. Poisonous ones. Containing illustrations."

I regarded the pile with some doubt.

"Ha!" Dodo sniped. "I can tell by your face you're not sure of the pertinence of these, and as and of themselves, there probably isn't much. Witches, wizards, warlocks— even fae—the world over study such books. There is nothing to fear inside these slender volumes."

He patted the pile beside them. "And these three little beauties are *The Witch's Guide to Common British Flowers*, *The Witch's Garden Companion* and *A Witch's Compendium of Useful Herbs*."

I waited, sure there would be more.

"Again. There's nothing here to concern us. Except ... in

all seven of these books there are notes written in the margins."

"Notes?" I asked.

"More accurately, I should say spells. Notes on spells. Fragments of spells."

"Uh-oh," said Snitch.

"Bad spells?" I ventured.

"The worst. Black spells. Spells that would do harm and wreak havoc were they complete."

"I see," I said.

"And then there was this beauty." With another flick of his finger, Dodo lifted a thin volume, probably no more than seven inches by five, in a faded cover, now a charcoal grey. There might once have been gold embossing but that had long faded, and all that was left now was a darker shape in the centre that might have been a bull or a minotaur.

It hovered just out of reach, and when I stretched a hand out to pluck it from the air, Dodo hurriedly drew it back to himself and deposited it on his desk.

"No touching," he snapped.

"Okay." *Prickly, or what?* "What is it?"

"I found it tucked inside a collection of children's comics." His tone had turned icy. "It's a black grimoire. One of the most destructive I have ever come across. Full of hate. Murder at its heart."

"A grimoire, like the kind you used to search out?" I asked. *And the reason why you were murdered in the first place?*

"Not *like* them!" Dodo exploded, spitting the words out vehemently. The book rose again, spinning in the air to the side of his head. "This, my dear, empty-headed detective, is one of the very items I had in my possession when I was murdered."

"But—" I stared at the spinning book—I didn't want to doubt him—before expelling a sharp peel of laughter, as though the whole matter was ridiculous. "Couldn't it simply be a different version? Something similar?"

"No," Dodo replied, snatching the book out of the air and slamming it down on his desk. "This isn't a duplicate! It isn't one that has been lost and somehow found! It's not a replica! It isn't a copy! It isn't even a photocopy! It's the original!"

I wrestled with what he was implying. "But that means—"

"It means that every bit of my hard work has been undone! My entire collection has been broken up and dispersed! All those years of hard graft, begging, borrowing, hiding from evil, outwitting the powerful, seeking out the worst our kind can dream up, then keeping those books safe or—more difficult still—finding ways to eradicate and destroy them. It was a gigantic waste of time! My lifetime's vocation, released back into the world like the evils in Pandora's box!"

"Uh-oh," said Snitch.

Uh-oh, indeed.

CHAPTER 10

I t was dark when I finally returned home.

I ambled through Peachstone Market, bustling with late-night shoppers, and barely noticed anyone else's existence. The air was fragranced with spice and incense, roasting meat and ground herbs; children were running around, dogs were barking. There was a folk band playing somewhere, adding to the liveliness of the evening, and yet I felt detached from the community, enclosed within a tomb of anxiety.

I could well understand Wizard Dodo's despair at finding the grimoire out in the wild. What a thankless, joyless task he had set himself. Tracking down endless volumes of evil, and for what? Just to have a serving detective stab him through the heart and ensure his lifetime's work amounted to naught.

I let myself into my flat, closing the door on the world with a sigh. This was home. Not much to speak of. A front door that opened into a narrow hallway. A boxy kitchen with barely enough room for two people to stand and converse. A small living room with a sofa, a television that I rarely watched, a couple of bookcases with books that I had yet to read, and a coffee table piled high with work that I needed to do.

My favourite room was the bedroom, and it was here that I spent most of my time, principally because I was only ever at home long enough to shower and sleep. I dumped my bag in the hallway, threw my leather jacket over a hook and dragged myself into the kitchen. Pulling open the fridge, I stared at its contents. Half a tin of tomatoes, some dried-out mushrooms and a couple of wrinkled bell peppers.

Pasta!

Unfortunately, my pasta tin only contained a couple of dusty crumbs of brittle dough, so I cancelled that idea and considered ordering in pizza, but instead opted for a frozen dinner. The freezer compartment was full of those. I slapped a ravioli in the microwave and headed for my shower. As the hot water thundered down, massaging my scalp and aching head, I pondered on the impossibility of maintaining law and order in a world such as ours. Too many people looking for an easy way to make money or exert power; too much greed and not enough moral fibre. Such thoughts made me sick to my stomach.

But they reminded me why I'd become a police officer in the first place.

Having discussed the situation at length with Dodo and the others in the office, eventually I'd felt it only right that I inform Monkton too. Like me, he'd been horrified by the news but, he wanted to know, was the appearance of the black grimoire pertinent to the tea party murders?

At this stage we couldn't know.

And neither could Monkton deal with Wizard Dodo's concerns about his collection being spread far and wide. The missing 'evidence' from Dodo's murder was not a concern for homicide, and my complaint about the misplaced items had more than likely been filed ...

And promptly lost.

Ibeus's ability to work at the higher echelons of the MOWPD hierarchy pointed to systemic corruption at the heart of the institutions we witches held dear.

It would take more than Dodo, Monkton or myself to clean that mess up.

Thoroughly disheartened, I sank into the comfy lounge chair by my bay window and stared out over the market. The crowds were beginning to disperse, heading for the shops, or home, or some other form of entertainment.

Picking at my ravioli, I watched the shadows, wondering as I always did about those creatures that moved among them, unknown and unknowable. The ghosts of Tumble Town's previous residents? Or something else?

I'd often marvelled at the notion that in Tumble Town, you could never be totally alone. The Shadow People infiltrated every corner, every nook and cranny. Alleys, open spaces, buildings, hallways. There was no hiding your secrets from these people. They were omnipresent. So much so, in fact, one had a tendency to forget their existence.

They must know so much, I told myself. Being party to every secret. If there had been a way to tap into that wealth of information, imagine how many crimes you could solve! How many arsonists and burglars and murderers you could apprehend! How many homicides you could prevent!

The thoughts swirled round and round in my brain, driving me crazy. So much so that I half considered heading back out in search of the nearest pub that would serve Blue Goblin vodka at this time of night. A tumbler full of vodka would offer temporary clarity.

A second one? Escape from reality.

But that's all it was. A consideration.

I dropped the idea quickly enough. Drowning my sorrows wouldn't get the tea party murderer or murderers off the street.

Far better to take care of myself and put in another hard day's graft tomorrow. Just before I tucked myself up in bed, I typed a short message to Monkton.

CP might know what happened to Dodo's collection.

CP. Cerys Pritchard. My ex-colleague. The person who had murdered Dodo.

I hadn't imagined Monkton would reply—he'd either be busy or asleep—but my phone beeped almost by return.

But she's incarcerated in Hawthorn West and she talks to NO-ONE.

She'd been moved from Witchity Grubbs, had she? I suppose it had only been a matter of time. Her mental state had broken down completely. They'd have wanted to move her for her own safety and for everyone else's.

Just a thought, I texted back.

How is this relevant to T Party case? Get some sleep, Liddell, was Monkton's response.

I lay on my side, eyes wide open, watching the shadows.

Who are you? I asked. *What stories could you tell? You*

helped me before. Helped me escape from Taurus's men. Won't you help me now?

If anyone or anything could read my thoughts, nothing responded.

It didn't matter; I was confident I could handle most situations. With a little luck and a following wind.

I couldn't clean up the whole of Tumble Town, but I could at least mop up one small corner of it.

———

"Ow! Ow! Ow!" I was plucking toast out of my toaster and burning my fingers when Monkton rang the next morning. I'd been up at first light, enjoyed a quick run and then thrown myself back into the shower. It wasn't even eight o'clock yet.

"You're early," I said in greeting. "I thought I was doing well."

"I've been at work for two hours, Liddell. That's the joy of being a DCI."

"Not much joy in it, is there?" I asked, peering inside the butter dish. If I scraped the insides there'd be just enough for two slices of toast. Yum. Stale bread is my absolute favourite.

Not.

"Did you get any sleep at all?" I asked, reaching for the marmite.

"Enough. Hold on." He covered the phone and I heard his muffled voice barking orders at some poor subordinate. "You still there?" he asked a moment later.

"Yes," I told him, wedging the phone between my ear

and my shoulder in order to spread the marmite on my toast. The butter had barely made it to the crusts and everything looked rather meagre. I really needed to go grocery shopping.

"Pritchard wants to see you," he said.

"What?" I dropped the knife I was holding and made a grab for my phone as it started to slip from my ear. "Have you spoken to her?" I asked, incredulous that he might have done so in the few hours between my text and this conversation.

"No. Have you?" I could hear an element of suspicion in his tone.

"No, of course not." I frowned. "I didn't even know she'd been moved from Witchity Grubbs."

"That's what I thought." He exhaled softly, as though he'd been holding on to some tension. "What's going on?" he asked.

I took a moment to consider my response. It was an ambivalent question, and without being able to see his face, I couldn't be entirely sure what he was asking. In the silence, my brain clicked and whirred through a dozen scenarios. I didn't like any of them.

"How secure is this line?" I asked. *How secure is anything in Tumble Town?*

"Come to the station," he told me. "Be here by nine. I'll drive you."

The Hawthorn West Hospital for the Criminally Insane was way out in the Berkshire countryside, ninety minutes' drive or so from London. Monkton was a safe pair of hands behind the wheel. He drove steadily and calmly, taking no risks, never venturing above the speed limit, aware of what was around him at all times. Soft jazz played on the radio. Perhaps that's what kept him so calm.

I had pulled my notebook and pen out of my bag and was ready to write down questions. "We need a strategy," I said. "Are we going for the usual good cop, bad cop routine or—"

"I'm not going in," Monkton said with a flicker of a smile, never taking his eyes from the road.

"What do you mean?"

"She doesn't want to talk to *me*."

"I don't suppose she'll do a lot of talking at all." I shrugged. "Since when was someone not wanting to talk to a police officer—and her old boss to boot—a reason for you not to try?"

"It's not about trying, though," Monkton told me. "She asked for *you*."

It took a moment for that to sink in. "*Asked* for me?"

"Mm-hm."

"If she asked for me, then that means she's got something she wants to tell me," I said. *Wow. That was a turn-up for the books.*

"Genius, Liddell."

"Alright, smart-arse." I bit down on the top of my pen. "So, what is my strategy then? Do I have one?"

"Do you need one? That's the question," Monkton replied. "One way to play it is simply to go in there and see what she wants. You can always come out again. You don't have to do or say anything. You certainly shouldn't agree to anything."

"True." I suddenly had an urge for coffee. I'd need fortifying to deal with Cerys. We'd been friends once. I peered out of the window, looking for a blue motorway services sign. There! Eleven miles.

"Can we stop?" I asked.

"Stop? We've only been on the road for ten minutes."

"More like twenty."

"Twelve, in fact."

"It feels like hours."

"Are you after coffee?" Monkton sounded exasperated. "Honestly, you need to curb that caffeine addiction of yours."

"I need a bathroom break," I replied primly, aware that the miles were passing and I didn't want him to zoom past the exit. "You don't want me to dampen your upholstery, do you?"

"It's not my upholstery—it's a pool car so I couldn't give a flying fig. I should imagine it's seen worse."

He had a point. These cars were signed out, utilised for all manner of jobs, and were used and abused in the worst possible ways. Most of them ended up scrapped sooner rather than later because there was no point selling them on.

"But if you insist." Monkton sighed. "We've just about got enough time if you don't dilly-dally."

"I won't," I promised, settling back for the last few miles before the exit, smiling inwardly.

He was still moaning when we parked up. "You'll have

to be quick. I'm worried we'll hit traffic as we approach Reading."

"Tell you what," I said, "if you're so worried, why don't I visit the ladies while you join the coffee queue?"

"I thought—"

"I'll have a triple expresso in a long cup with milk and two sugars. Thank you." I jumped from the car and raced away before he could protest any further. By the time I'd attended to business and dried my hands on one of those air dryers that practically peel the skin from your bones, Monkton had almost made it to the front of the queue. I eyed the brownies thoughtfully, then as he was about to pay, plonked one on the counter.

"Oi," he said.

"My sugar levels are a bit low."

"Get out."

"Is that everything?" the long-suffering till operator asked him.

Monkton turned the brownie in its cellophane wrapping over. "Are these vegetarian, do you know?" he asked the operator.

She shrugged, neither knowing nor caring by the look of it. I quickly scanned the ingredients. "Yep." I slid another one onto the countertop, Monkton paid and, grabbing our drinks—he opted for tea—we made our way outside.

It was a grim day. The sky was overcast, threatening rain. Little specks of drizzle pecked at my face, but not enough that I needed to worry about my lack of umbrella. In some ways it was refreshing to be away from London. I tended to forget just how claustrophobic Tumble Town could be, and after a weekend in Devon, where the sky stretched away forever, I felt it more than ever.

Monkton stopped dead suddenly. When I turned to look at him, he jerked his head towards some tables. It was hardly the weather to sit outside and enjoy our break, but I followed him anyway and took a seat opposite him when he sat down.

"What's up?" I asked. "I thought you were in a hurry."

"*We're* in a hurry," he reminded me. "Your pass is for eleven. I don't want you to miss it."

"So, why are we—?"

He placed a finger on his lips and I shut up. "That's nice," he said. "Let me enjoy the silence for a moment."

When I offered him a little deadeye, he sighed. "We need to understand the bigger picture," he said. "And at the moment I can't get a handle on anything."

I nodded, understanding immediately what he was driving at. "Is the tea party connected to the Labyrinthians' case?"

"Exactly." He looked around, almost casually, observing the people who milled around us. The motorway service was busy, as you'd expect, but not so chock-a-block that we wouldn't notice any unusual onlookers.

"You're worried that our conversations are being overheard?" I asked.

He nodded. "How do we go from two short texts about Pritchard last night to you being invited to see her this morning?"

I couldn't explain that. It made me uneasy too.

"And about that?" he continued. "Is it merely coincidence, or are there links that we're not seeing?"

"The black grimoire turning up at Fletcher Gate? That's the biggest indicator of a link to me," I said.

He nodded. "I agree. I also believe that someone wanted to get rid of everyone around that table in one fell swoop."

"That would make sense if we were all police officers," I said. "Even if some of those there weren't involved in law and order in some way, there must be a reason why the Labyrinthians would want us out of the way."

"And Ibeus?" Monkton asked.

"I don't know." That was puzzling me. "Perhaps she'd crossed them. Betrayal of some kind? Outlived her usefulness? Could be anything, couldn't it?" I thought again about Wesley Warthog. "And what about Warthog? Perhaps he was a supplier of some kind. Or maybe he overheard something? Knew inside information—"

"Eight dead. One seriously ill. Your mate a no-show—"

"I wouldn't call Culpeper my mate," I reasoned.

"I hope not, given that he's a prime suspect at the moment."

"What?" I jerked away from him.

"Oh, hadn't you heard?" he asked, almost casually. "Even the MOWPD have one or two units looking for him. Strictly on the quiet."

I caught my breath. "Why?"

"The word is out that he should have been in attendance."

"That doesn't make him guilty of multiple homicides!"

"Clearly." Monkton shifted under my glare. "But given that he can't be found ..."

"You haven't found any trace of him, have you?" I asked, thinking of Minsk.

"No," Monkton replied, his voice flat. "And we're not going to, are we? The Dark Squad know what they're doing."

"Do you think they're covering for him?" I couldn't see that myself.

"Who knows." Monkton sniffed and toyed with his cardboard takeaway cup.

"You and me make twelve," I reminded him. "Then there's the one that got away." I blinked and caught my breath. "Oh, dang and blast."

"What?"

"Snitch! I was so bogged down in what Wizard Dodo was telling me yesterday that I didn't follow up on what *he* had to tell me." I glanced at my watch. Snitch wouldn't be awake yet. "I'll have to catch up with him later." Today was going to be as exhausting as yesterday. I took a big slug of my coffee.

"Be careful of what you say, where you say it and to whom you're speaking," Monkton said, then gestured in the direction of the car. "And that includes Pritchard."

I nodded and pushed my seat back. "Let's go."

Chapter 11

The Hawthorn West Hospital for the Criminally Insane might as well have been Witchity Grubbs in the countryside. Once upon a time it had been a Victorian prison housing low-life felons, an overspill from the infamous Reading gaol where Oscar Wilde had been incarcerated. It had been decommissioned in the 1930s but pressed back into use during the Second World War to house enemy officers, diplomats and anyone else deemed to be an adversary or a threat to the British people. After being allowed to fall into disrepair, the Ministry of Witches had bought the building from the British government in the 1950s and used it as a hospital. Ostensibly that's what it remained.

A hospital, but a highly secure one.

Just the sight of it made me shiver. Witchity Grubbs was bad enough, but this building even managed to lack what character the London prison had. The structure had been created using grey stone and slate. The windows were uniform, each exactly the same size as its neighbours, small and boxy with bars criss-crossing each. There were no turrets, nothing decorative at all. The grand entrance, where once horses would pull carts and carriages through, was a façade. Nowadays, the way in was through a pair of simple glass doors to each side. Women to the left, men to the right. CCTV cameras hung from brackets all around the building and, as we turned into the car park, several swivelled to take a good long look at us.

Monkton parked the car in the first available bay. "I'll wait here," he said.

I grabbed my ID but left the rest of my belongings with him, bar my notebook and a pencil. I knew the authorities wouldn't allow anything else through, not with the evident need for security in a place like this. A small camera trained itself on me as I approached the glass door. I waved my PI licence upwards, and a few seconds later, the glass door swept open.

I stepped through into a world of white. A white tiled floor. White walls. Staff in white uniforms. What wasn't white was made of glass or some kind of super-tough Perspex. A gap appeared in a window to the right of me and a pair of eyes inspected me. "Help you?" a voice asked.

"Elise Liddell," I said, handing my licence over to be scrutinised. "I had a call about one of your inmates—"

"Patients," the woman said.

"Beg your pardon, patients."

"Cerys Pritchard, was it?" the woman asked, and slid my licence back to me.

"That's right."

"Okay. Take this." She handed me a pass on a lanyard. It was luminous yellow with a big black V on it. It stood out against all the white. "You need to go through the door on the left behind you. Security will pat you down and take you through to a visiting room."

I nodded my thanks and did as I was told. On the other side of the next door, security consisted of half a dozen burly guards, the tallest and broadest of whom was a woman named Officer Ryan, who quickly and efficiently searched me, confiscated my notebook and handed me some paper instead.

"You can have your notebook back when you come out," she said. "I doubt you'll be long."

I regarded her uncertainly. "How come?"

"She never says a word, that Pritchard. You can't even blame it on the drugs, because she isn't prescribed that many. Not like some in here."

"I see."

"Are you ready?" she asked me.

"I am," I confirmed.

"I should take this opportunity to remind you that you are not allowed to hand the patient anything, including your pencil or paper. You must not touch the patient. You should alert staff if the patient becomes agitated. Do not attempt to placate the patient or calm her down if she becomes reactive."

"Okay," I agreed.

"If the patient becomes verbally aggressive or otherwise aggravated or unhappy, starts to cry or shout, rock, slap or punch herself or her surroundings, you should back away. You must leave any subsequent interaction to our welfare officers or security. Is that understood?"

"Yes."

"Very well." She handed me a clipboard. "Sign here"—she flipped the page over—"and here."

I followed her instructions.

Finally, Officer Ryan led me through a set of locked double doors. Unlike Witchity Grubbs, Hawthorn West had been completely modernised. There were no clanking gates here, no clinking keys on the end of chains. Here, everything was operated by an invisible person in a control room somewhere. Small cameras followed my every movement. Once past the second door, I was x-rayed, sniffed by a spaniel and finally escorted to a visiting room. Much like the ones in Witchity Grubbs, this was a small square room housing two chairs, both bolted to the floor, and a table. The walls were constructed from glass, or as before, a heavy clear Perspex, something of the kind.

"Take a seat," Officer Ryan instructed me. "She'll be along in a minute."

I waited alone, notepaper and pencil on the table in front of me, trying not to fidget, slightly anxious that Cerys would change her mind. I took time to study my surroundings—not that there was anything much to see. A small camera in two corners that would be able to capture anything untoward. No doubt there were microphones in here too. Nothing we discussed in this room would be private. The lights above hummed and buzzed. I tipped my head back, gazing upwards, mildly irritated, and realised that unlike the rest of the refurbished décor, they were still the old fluorescent lights, the kind that become yellow with age.

Seven or eight minutes later, I heard the door at the far end of the corridor swish open, and I sat up, waiting to see who would appear. Officer Ryan and a colleague, flanking a woman barely recognisable to me. At first I assumed they had the wrong person, but as they strolled closer, I could see this *was* Cerys, albeit a sadder version of my ex-colleague.

The doors swished open and she was led inside. Without looking at me, she slid into the seat opposite and waited patiently, head drooping, while Officer Ryan's colleague secured the chains to a loop on the floor.

Officer Ryan pointed at a strip on the wall. "Push this in case of emergency," she told me. "But we'll only be outside."

"Thank you," I said, and crossed my hands in my lap, waiting for them to leave.

They took up positions outside, backs to us, and once the room was still, I studied the woman opposite me.

Not so very long ago, she'd been a pretty thing, with typical Welsh colouring. Dark chocolate eyes and hair as black and sleek as a raven's wing, cropped in an attractive bob. The last time I'd seen her, the stress had been beginning to show. Her hair had started to grey; her face was lined. She'd lost an awful lot of weight. Now she was bloated, far beyond any weight I'd known her to be. Her white and clammy skin had become pockmarked, rather like the underside of a long-dead fish. The black beneath her eyes seemed permanent now, and her hair had turned completely white.

Officer Ryan had suggested Cerys wasn't being prescribed many drugs, yet what else could have caused this change in her appearance? Here was a woman with the burden of her past deeds weighing on her shoulders, and it wasn't a pretty sight.

"Hello, Cerys," I said, keeping my voice neutral. The last time I'd seen her, I'd driven the body blow, informing her of the murder of Kevin Makepeace, her boyfriend. It hadn't gone down well. I had the feeling that this might be payback time if I didn't play my cards right.

She still refused to acknowledge me, remaining so motionless I could almost believe she hadn't heard me speak, didn't register my existence even.

Almost.

"Cut the crap, Cerys." My voice was sharp. "You asked me to come and I don't have a great deal of time, so let's get to it." *Whatever* it *is*.

Finally, her gaze shifted, a small half-smile playing on her dry lips as she regarded me from beneath sparse brows. "I wasn't sure you'd bother to come," she said, and her voice sounded harsh and husky, as though she hadn't used it for a long time.

"You summon me and I appear. I am your genie in the bottle." There was no hiding my sarcasm. "The thing is, Cerys, I'm a busy woman. I'm not here to play games."

"Was Monkton peeved that I didn't want to see him?" she asked.

I shrugged one shoulder. I made it a rule never to give away any information about my colleagues. You never knew what could be used against them.

"I'll bet he was," she continued, speaking almost to herself. She laughed. A rusty cog in need of greasing.

I kept my gaze steady. "I didn't come here to talk about DCI Wyld," I told her.

"But it's nice to get one over on him." She smiled at me. I noticed she had a couple of teeth missing. How had that happened? Was she being mistreated? "But of course, you wouldn't do that. You always were his golden girl." She spoke these words without the slightest hint of malice, just matter of fact.

"Can we cut to the chase?" I asked.

"Because you're absurdly busy, aren't you, Elise?" She hissed on the final syllable of my name, drawing it out, enjoying how it sounded. "What with villains and murders and tea parties and things of that kind."

My blood froze. *She knew about the tea party*! This was beyond what either Monkton or I had anticipated.

"What do you know?" I asked.

"Ooh! See how your green eyes widened at that, Elise!" She snickered, and it was the most insane sound I'd ever heard. No genuine merriment, just something dark and twisted.

"Tell me about the tea party," I said.

She leaned in towards me and the smile disappeared, her eyes hard and black. "You're not here to make demands, Elise. This is my show."

I felt my eye twitch. Monkton had said to walk out, take time to consider what was being said, but Cerys had already pulled the proverbial rug out from under my feet. I was all ears, and she knew it.

"Go on," I said.

She nodded in satisfaction. "I *can* tell you things, for sure."

"What things?"

"Oh come, come." She looked disappointed. "At the moment, I hold all the cards and you have none. If I tell you what I know, then what can I bargain with? That's not how this is going to work."

"So you're willing to tell me things?" I asked her. "You're willing to talk to me now?"

She nodded.

I leaned back in my chair, subconsciously trying to create more space between us. "What's changed?" I asked her. "You never wanted to talk to me before."

"I wasn't in my right mind before," she told me. "Now I am."

I must have looked incredulous because the corner of her mouth curled. "You're no shrink, Elise, so it's probably best if you don't try to psychoanalyse me."

I sighed. "Fair enough. I'll take your word for it then. You're sane, and now you want to provide me with information."

"That's about the size of it."

"But you know I need to have some idea of what information you have before I agree to anything."

"You're fishing."

"Obviously." I frowned. "I have a job to do. You don't think you're going to lead me blindly into some agreement when I'm not even convinced you can deliver?"

"I can deliver." Her hard little eyes glared at me, her mouth set in a firm line. "The question really is how badly do you want what I have?"

I lay my hands on the table, palms down. "I don't know what you can possibly tell me that I don't already know," I told her. "You murdered Wizard Dodo. You did so at the behest of the Labyrinthians. What else is there to say?"

"Tch-ch-ch-ch-ch." Again, the disappointed face. "Please stop, Elise. You're putting our profession to shame."

"Our profession." I rolled my eyes. "We're at an impasse, Cerys. If you won't even hint at what you know, then I'm out of here." I drew my chair back.

She levelled a gaze at me that ten years ago might have made my insides shrivel. But I was no nice, naive PC anymore. I'd come up against bigger and better than Cerys in my time at the MOWPD. "You leave, and more people die," she told me, her mouth curling in grim satisfaction.

"More police officers? Is that what we're doing here?" I pushed my chair backwards. "Making threats? Death threats? Because if it is, we have nothing more to say to each other. Mark my words, I will do everything in my power to make sure you never see the light of day again."

As I stood, I saw a flicker of genuine emotion cross her face for the first time. *Fear?* I paused. Officer Ryan, sensing movement, turned around. When she saw me on my feet, she glanced up at the camera beside the door. I held my hand up, indicating everything was fine, and slowly sat down again.

Perhaps I needed to approach this from a different angle.

"What is it you want?" I asked, and this time the smile on Cerys's face was one of triumph.

She took a deep breath. "I know I'm never getting out of prison," she said. "Not for what I've done. I'm pretty certain that the Ministry of Witches would happily throw me into the darkest of dungeons and allow me to rot without so much as a second thought."

She was probably right.

"But if I have to live the rest of my life incarcerated, I'd like to do it in a certain amount of comfort."

Here it comes, I thought.

"I want to be moved."

Of course she did. "Back to Witchity Grubbs?" *Why would anyone want to go back there?*

"No. I want to go to one of those semi-open prisons. The women-only ones. Like Bassaleg." She named a prison on the outskirts of Cardiff. "Or Belhus Wood." The closest to Tumble Town.

I could hardly hide my scepticism. "You know, Cerys ... I don't have anything like the authority to grant a wish like that."

"Of course I know that," she snapped impatiently. "But you have the *ear* of people who do. And you can be very persuasive."

I wasn't sure whether either of those things were true, but I certainly wasn't one to give up until I'd had my way. Tenacious? Yes. That probably described what I am.

"And the thing is," she continued, "I'll only tell *you*, so they needn't try to send in any of their bigwigs. Or Wyld, for that matter." Poor Monkton. She dismissed him so easily.

I paid careful attention to her body language. She wasn't giving anything away, but you know me. I'm suspicious by nature. She was oddly still and assured. "Why *only* me?" I asked.

"Because this is personal for you," she said.

I gave a minute shake of my head.

"Don't pretend it isn't. You got yourself all tied up in knots about who killed your wizard. Then you were all het up because it was me, someone you liked and respected.

You beat yourself up when bad things happen to your friends—"

"I'm a professional," I reminded her, but she laughed me off.

"We both know you're an *emotional* being. You can't separate the professional from the personal, and you don't want to. That's why you fell so hard after Ezra was killed."

I waved her explanation away. "So you say. The thing is, no-one is going to listen to me. You know I don't work for the MOWPD anymore. I hold no sway. Contrary to what you think, I don't have anyone's ear."

"Believe me, Elise." She leaned forward once more and beamed her mirthless grin. "They'll want to listen to you when they know I can blow the whole Labyrinthian thing wide open."

My heart rate shot up. There! She'd actually insinuated she could tell us all we needed to know about one of the most feared underground organisations known to the MOWPD.

I shook my head again, pretending I didn't believe her, fighting to maintain my relaxed posture, sitting well back on the chair, fighting to quell my rising excitement.

"I know about Ibeus's involvement," she said.

I shrugged. "It's not a secret."

"There are others."

"Other ... police officers?"

She met my eyes, nodded once.

"Beat officers?" I pressed.

Again, a single nod. "And higher up."

That would be another reason why she wouldn't want to talk to higher-ranking officers, I assumed. But that left me in a quandary. How did I talk someone into meeting her demands if I didn't know who could be trusted?

I mentally shook myself. What was I thinking? There was nothing to negotiate. Cerys needed to remain locked up for a long, long time.

Taking a moment, I picked up the notepaper I'd laid out in front of me, folding it once, then again into quarters.

"I want to be able to walk outside," Cerys said, her voice slightly querulous now. "I miss the outdoors. It's inhumane to keep someone within four walls day after day for the rest of their lives."

I could understand that. It would drive me stir-crazy. But if you can't do the time, then don't do the crime.

"If the powers that be have assessed you as criminally insane then there's no way you're going anywhere," I reminded her.

"I'm being reassessed. I'm not even on too many meds anymore. I'm stable."

I pressed my lips together.

"I am," she insisted. "The doctors know that. They can't keep me locked up here if I'm not insane. I just need the Ministry of Witches to grant me a little clemency, and then I can be moved."

"I'm sorry," I told her. "I'm not the person to help you with this."

"You're exactly the person!" Cerys cried, slamming her hand on the table. The abruptness of her change of mood startled me. Her raised voice attracted the attention of Officer Ryan and her colleague. Both of them turned around to stare into the room.

"You need to calm down," I warned Cerys.

She lowered her voice. "I can help you bring the Labyrinthians down."

Silence.

"I can give you the Labyrinthians."

Outside, the officers were considering their options. Officer Ryan glanced at her watch.

"I know where you can find them."

"That's total BS!" I snapped, hoping to get one last rise from her.

She smirked and relaxed into her chair. "Then you'll never know, will you, Elise? Can you live with that?"

"Give me something," I said. "Prove to me that you know what you say you do."

She glanced over her shoulder and made eye contact with Officer Ryan. "We're done!" she called.

"Cerys ..." I tried once more, but she dropped her head and disengaged from me.

I looked on, helpless, as the officers began the process of releasing her from the bolts and chains. Cerys's face remained coldly neutral the whole time, and she said nothing as they led her away down the corridor, leaving me to stew in my own juice.

Monkton was pacing the length of the car park, his mobile clamped to his ear, when I eventually returned to him. All the security measures had to be run through again, this time in reverse, so that I could leave the hospital. It took some time.

"There you are!" he exclaimed as I trotted up to him.

"Sorry!" I followed as he hurried back to the car.

"We need to get back!" He jumped behind the steering wheel, and I barely had time to do my seatbelt up before he'd started the engine and was zooming out of the car park, despite the signs instructing us to drive at 10 mph.

"What's the rush?" I asked, putting a hand out to stop myself flying through the dashboard.

"Our tea party survivor just woke up."

CHAPTER 12

We sat in the car outside the hospital, Monkton sending a text to one of his team.

We'd been through my interview with Cerys over and over again, analysing it from every angle.

"She's smart," Monkton said, slipping his phone back into the inside pocket of his jacket. It pinged almost immediately. In fact, Monkton's phone hadn't stopped pinging and ringing since I'd rejoined him. He was constantly in demand.

"Yes," I agreed. "Not quite so insane as we all assumed."

"Pulling *you* in rather than a serving officer means that nothing she says is admissible. You can't caution her, and anything she does divulge would probably be thrown out as inadmissible due to hearsay."

"What's her likelihood of being moved to a semi-open prison if she *is* reassessed and classified as sane?" I asked.

"It won't happen," Monkton replied. "Not if the Ministry have anything to say about it. And they will. A serving police officer? Even if Ibeus hadn't betrayed the force, they'd have taken a dim view of Pritchard's trans-gressions."

"I suppose we have to let someone above our paygrade in on it?" I asked.

"Above my paygrade, you mean," Monkton grunted. "I wasn't aware that detective agency of yours was actually making much money."

"It ticks over." The way a clock that's been trodden on by an elephant ticks over.

"Mmm. I'll run it past Burns, see what he thinks should be done." Pete Burns. Monkton's new and probably temporary boss. One of those ambitious young graduates making a name for himself. "He'll send it further up the food chain if needs be, but I honestly doubt anything will come from this."

"That's what I thought you'd do," I agreed. "I can't quite get over the fact that she knew about the tea party. Even inside a secure unit like Hawthorn West."

"You'd be amazed ..."

I sighed. "So what now?"

"What now?" Monkton poked his thumb in the direc-tion of the hospital's main entrance. "We go in and inter-view our survivor."

Monkton flashed his warrant card at reception—his opened all doors in a way that my PI licence didn't—and we were directed up in the lift to the fifth floor. "Apparently they have him on a side ward," Monkton told me. "They were assuming he wouldn't make it, so wanted him to have privacy."

"Any family?" I asked.

"Nope."

"Shame. I wouldn't want to die alone," I said.

"I'd rather die alone in a side room than have a dozen other people moaning and groaning and asking for bedpans in my immediate vicinity," Monkton said.

I grinned at that, moving to the side as we stopped on the second floor. The doors opened and a little girl on a trolley was wheeled inside, her mum trailing after her, clutching half a dozen brand new soft toys. The little girl had a bandage wrapped around her hand, swelling it to the size of a basketball.

"Oh no!" I said, purely conversationally while we waited for the porters to sort themselves out and get the lift going again. "What did you do?"

"Mind your own business," the kid told me, scowling in contempt. My mouth dropped open in surprise. She must have been six at the most.

Monkton had a sudden coughing fit.

"Margarita!" Mum scolded.

"It's fine," I reassured her. "I was being nosy."

"She fell off her bike," Mum told me.

"Oh dear, sorry about that," I said to Margarita. "I hope you're all fixed soon."

"You look like a witch," Margarita told me.

"Margarita!" Mum flushed a bright pink. "I'm so sorry."

"Are you a witch?" the kid demanded to know.

"She sure is," said Monkton and coughed again.

"Can you fix my wrist?" the girl asked, holding up her arm.

"She's not that good at magick," said Monkton.

We stopped at our floor and stepped out. "I'm a detective, not a surgeon," I told her apologetically. "But you ought to know, if you *ever* murder someone, I will find you and, make no mistake, I will lock you up for the whole of your natural life."

The doors slid closed, shutting off my view of the aghast faces of the porters, Mum and little Margarita.

"Was that entirely necessary?" Monkton asked.

I smiled. "I think so."

"She was only curious."

I harrumphed. "You know what curiosity did to the cat, don't you?"

Tutting, Monkton set off down the corridor.

I reset my halo and traipsed after him.

———

"Wizard Hornswoggler?" Monkton approached the bed, where a nurse was busy fiddling with lines and machines and all manner of things that I had no knowledge of. I'm sure if I did have, I'd have been able to fix young Margarita's wrist right up, but there you go. "Hari Hornswoggler?"

The old man lying on the bed opened his eyes and blinked a few times. Clean shaven, he had a bald head, his hair having migrated to his eyebrows—they were the bushiest I'd ever seen—and a wonderfully hooked nose. His arms were outside the covers, his good left hand covering the end of the stump at his right wrist. "Who's that?" he asked.

"DCI Monkton Wyld," said Monkton, flashing his warrant card, "and DI Elise Liddell." I held up my PI licence.

"Eurgh." The wizard turned his face away. "I don't want nuffink to do wiv the bizzies."

Oh. It was going to be like that, was it?

The nurse smiled at me. "He's a little bit more spirited than he was in ICU," she said.

"Wizard Hornswoggler?" I stepped forward so he could see me more clearly. "How are you feeling?" I didn't wait for him to reel off all the reasons he was feeling like sheep poop; I could tell by his yellowy-grey skin texture and the hollows in his cheeks that he had been, and probably still was, extremely sick. "It must be quite a shock for you to wake up in hospital this way."

"I can't deny that," the wizard agreed. "I'd rather go home, but they say I can't."

"Not yet." I smiled warmly, turning on the charm offensive. "Not till they've made sure you're well on the way to recovery."

He sighed, seeming totally despondent. "What happened? Why am I here?"

"Nobody's told you?" I asked.

"No-one's told me nuffink!" the wizard snarled, glaring at the nurse who was entirely unperturbed. "They just poke me and prod me and stick needles in me. They've turned me into a pin cushion, they 'ave! It's not on!"

Stepping right up to the foot of the bed, I asked, "Do you remember the tea party?"

"Tea party?" He frowned in confusion. "Tea party ... wait ..." His eyes widened as he began to remember. "Yes ... yes. The tea party."

The nurse had finished doing whatever she was doing, and stepped out of the way. "Take a seat," she said, and I pulled a chair around to sit alongside the wizard. Monkton grabbed a spare from the other bed. Hornswoggler had the benefit of a two-person room while being the only occupant, so we weren't in danger of being overheard.

"What happened at the tea party?" he asked, and now he sounded anxious. "How did I end up here?"

"We were hoping you could tell us," I said, reaching out to smooth his hand. Despite being no fan of the police, he allowed me to. His skin was paper thin and dry. I stroked it softly.

"You remind me of my daughter," he told me, rheumy eyes suddenly glistening.

His daughter? Hadn't Monkton only this minute told me the old fellow had no family? "Has anyone called her for you?" I asked. "I could—"

"No. No. She went away a long time ago. I haven't seen her ..." His voice trailed off. Worried we'd lost him altogether, I leaned closer, squeezing his hand. "Must be thirty years," he said. "Near as. She had pink hair."

I glanced up at Monkton and he pulled his finger across his throat and shook his head.

Oh. Shame.

"Is there anyone else?" I asked, wondering where he would go once he was well enough.

"Nah. Just me neighbours." He sniffed. Struggled to sit up a little. "So, what do you people want?"

"Can you tell us about the party?" Monkton asked again. "Whatever you remember might be helpful to us."

"Not sure I want to be spillin' me guts to the bizzies ..."

"The thing is, Wizard Hornswoggler ..." I tried to pick my words with care, and then decided a blunt approach might be better. "There were thirteen people invited to that tea party, and eight of them are dead."

The wizard's face blanched even whiter than previously. "Is that true?" His chin wobbled.

I nodded.

He sank further into his pillow. "I knew it."

Monkton leaned forward. "You knew it?"

The wizard nodded slowly. "Can I have some water?" he asked. "My mouth is so dry."

Monkton filled a glass from the jug on the bedside table. There was a straw too, which was useful. As I raised the wizard up, Monkton held the straw in front of his lips. Hari sucked a little, swallowed, and took some more.

"Better?" I asked and he nodded.

"Eight dead?"

"Yes." I softly lowered his head. "I'm sorry. Did you know anyone there?"

His gaze turned inwards and he took his time to think. "Yes. Yes, I knew some of the people there."

"Do you know who sent you the invite?" I asked.

Now his eyes clouded over. "No. I mean. Not really."

Monkton's voice cut in. "But you went anyway?"

"What's it to ya?" the wizard growled in response.

I frowned at Monkton. "We were taken in too," I pointed out.

Monkton glared back at me. "Don't remind me."

The wizard regarded us with renewed interest. "You was supposed to be there?"

"Yes," I told him. "We were both delayed so we didn't make it for the start, and when we arrived it was already too late. To be honest," I admitted, "we thought you were a goner too."

Wizard Hornswoggler raised his impressively bushy eyebrows. "You found me?"

I nodded. "Alive."

"But only just," Monkton added.

The wizard whistled. "I owe you, then. Bizzies or not."

"You don't owe us," I told him. "We were just doing our jobs."

"That's as maybe, but old Hari is grateful for it." He patted my hand. "In return, I s'pose I'd better tell you what I know," he said. "Lift me up a bit, can you?"

I used the controls to lift the head of the bed and rearranged his pillows to make him more comfortable. After taking another sip of water, he began.

I was in Snakecharmers Lane when I got the invite. Visitin' Old Witch Lies-a-lot. Well, 'er real name is Lieselot, German or something, innit? But it's all the same, and Lies-a-Lot is pretty much what she does. But she also makes bloody good fish stew and that really 'elps with me rheumatics. Ooh, I suffers terrible, I does. It don't cost much, neither, her fish stew, cos she uses the odds and ends that no-one else wants and given her proximity to Dead Man's Wharf, she gets her stock for virtually nuffink. I lives on her stew, I really does. I'm a coeliac so it's hard for me. I can't eat bread and pies and fings ... turn me insides outside if I does.

Anyway, I'd been 'angin' about, shootin' the breeze with a couple of old fellows I know, waitin' for Lies-a-Lot to fill me flask, and this old dear walks past, draggin' a shoppin' trolley. I'd never seen her before, which, when you think about it, ain't so strange. I ain't suggestin' I know everyone in Tumble Town after all.

Tho' I do know a lot of people, you can't deny that.

So she walks past me and ... if I remember right, there was a bit of a ruckus at the other end of the lane, the end nearest the wharf. Sounded like someone had dropped summink they shouldn't 'ave. Quite a crash. So, me old buddies set off in that direction to have a look, maybe see if they could rehome anything, on the sly, if you know what I mean ... but this old dear, there was summink about 'er ...

So I'm taking half a step after me mates and then another step after this woman and I'm dancin'. Dancin' in the middle of the lane. Whoop, this way, whoop that way. You know, givin' it a good jig.

But she pays me no mind, just carries on draggin' that trolley up the lane away from me, headin' further into Tumble Town and away from the river.

I can't explain why I just stood there, not quite paralysed, cos I could still move, but sort of ... sort of hypnomotised. That's what I was. Hypnomotised.

And then she dropped this envelope ... and I called out to her, I says, 'Hey lady!' but she kept on goin'. At that point, it's not that I came to my senses cos I would argue I was never out of them, but I managed to go after her and I bent down to retrieve said object, and when I looked up, waving it at her, like some demented postie, she'd gone.

Now you may call me crazy, right, but I swear, that envelope was addressed to me. At the time I never even considered it weird, cos, we live in a weird world and these is weird times. But it 'ad my name on it and I figured it belonged to me.

I can see by the way you're lookin' at me, young lady, that you know exactly what I'm talkin' about. Right?

Anyhoo ... so I ripped it open, and it's an invite to a function for retired chippies—that's carpenters to the uninitiated like you two—which is what I did in my younger days before I lost me 'and in an unfortunate workshop accident.

After that I couldn't work and I fell on hard times and me wife left me and it all went to pot really. I been doin' odd jobs n stuff for people, where I can, like, but I'm not nambi-dextrous enough to cope with hammers and saws. I was 'opin' me old gaffer would see his way to givin' me a bit of pension but the useless old bogger refused. Only finks of 'eself.

So, when I sees that the invite is from the Charitable League for Retired and Needy Magickal Carpenters, I thinks to meself, that's perfect, Hari! Perfect! Maybe they can give me an 'and, so to speak. An 'and out, rather than a prostfetic limb anyway, cos I tried one of them and I just couldn't get on with it.

So later that day, when was that? Yesterday? Two days ago? Jeepers! I 'ave been out of it, ain't I? I dressed up in me best robe and off I went. They did save that robe, did they? They didn't cut it off of me or nuffink stupid? Cost me an arm and a leg that did. Not literally, thank the goddess, else

I'd really be in trouble. Wouldn't be much of me left, would there?

Anyhoo, anyhoo ... I trots over to Fletcher Gate at the specified time. Nice gaff. Tres posh. Rings the doorbell and no-one comes. Aye-aye, Hari lad, *I thinks to meself.* Summink's not right 'ere, *and y'know, I almost turned round and went home, but I've got me gladrags on and if there's any chance I could get a bit of wonga, any chance at all, I want in. So I turns the door handle and lets meself in and there's this dead sophisticated hallway and the dining room beyond. You know about that, do ya? Oh, I s'pose you would, yeah. Yeah.*

Yeah, I was first there. No-one else at that stage. No-one from the charity and no waiting staff. And yet, the fires was lit, and the table was laid and there was tea and wine and cake and sarnies and it all looked dead impressive. I found me name on a card where I was supposed to be sitting.

I was on me best behaviour—I really was—although it did cross me mind that the candlesticks might be worth summink. But I was curious too, y'know? Where was everyone?

And then this woman came, and she eyed me like I was summink on the bottom of 'her shoe, I 'ave no idea who she was. Never seen her before. She thought she was better than me, though, the way she stared down her nose at me.

Describe her? Yeah, older woman. Really short hair.

Fortunately, some other people arrive then, and the thing is, I know two of 'em. The hatter chappie ... what's 'is name? Warthog? Yeah. That's 'im. Not much of an 'atter by all accounts, but I know of 'im. And 'is friend Maizie Thistle-bristle.

So then I know summink ain't right. This ain't a meeting

of chippies, and that was confirmed when old Tuttlewhirl turned up, cos everyone knows he's a retired copper. So what's going on?

We're all standin' around lookin' at each other and someone—one of the ones I don't know, and 'he's really well spoken, not Tumble Town born and bred like the rest of us— he says, 'maybe it will all become clear' or summink like that, and he suggests we all sit down and tuck in.

Maizie don't like that, cos there's some people ain't arrived, so she's all agitated and says it's bad manners, but then this other guy—and I know I've seen him somewhere before—he agrees cos he had to be somewhere else. Maizie says, 'alright, alright, you can start, but I won't.' She's got manners, you see. Well brought up, not dragged up like some. So we all sit down, except Maizie, and someone starts pourin' tea and people are asking questions about who each of us is, and some of 'em start snackin' on stuff and I 'as a look but I can't eat none of it! I mean, there's not even crisps or carrot sticks or somethin'. I'm well peeved, I can tell you.

Maizie goes out to check if anyone else is comin' and then, I think, yeah, the clocks start chimin' and stuff and the bloke I thought I knew says, 'Oh, I have to be in court in an hour so best hurry', and I'm sippin' my tea ... and I hear someone gasp ... and then there was a thud, someone falling on the floor, and I felt funny. Kind of heavy.

That's it.

That's all I remember.

Hari lapsed into silence, his pallid cheeks sinking, his lips almost grey. It had taken a lot to tell his story.

Monkton and I exchanged glances. So much to unpick. Where to start.

"This Maizie Thistlebristle," I said. "Can you tell me a little more about her? What does she look like? Where does she live?"

"She's ..." Hari blinked. "I don't know. She's average."

"Average?" I repeated. "Average height, weight?"

"Yeah, a bit round. She's not young. Forties, maybe."

"Hair colour?"

"Oh, I dunno. Never noticed. Brown, I s'pose. A little unkempt most of the time." He waved his good hand weakly. "And don't ask me what her bleedin' eye colour is cos I've never looked at her that closely. She'd be liable to slap me anyway."

"Feisty, is she?" Monkton asked.

"Don't suffer fools, that's for sure."

"And where does she live?"

"Dunno. Somewhere round Cockington Lane cos that's how she knows old Warthog, I s'pose." He turned to me. "You're talkin' about her in the present tense. She ain't—?"

"We only found one woman at the scene," I told him, thinking of the figure Snitch had seen running away. Could it have been a woman? We'd assumed it was male but that was a rookie mistake on my part, and I didn't recall Snitch saying one way or the other. "The description of the snooty woman you first spoke to would fit her."

"Awww." Hari smiled briefly. "I'm glad it weren't Maizie."

Never mind about Ibeus, though, I noted. Turns out she wasn't popular in any of her guises.

"Did you see a tall, extremely thin gentleman?" I asked, thinking of Culpeper. "Very pale. Tidy facial hair? Long, slim fingers with ... erm ... odd nails?" I wiggled my fingers, as though that would prompt Hari's memory of Culpeper's peculiarly discoloured nails.

"Can't say I did." Hari shrugged. "Weren't no-one partickerly tall. And everyone who was there looked like they'd been at 'ome fer mealtimes."

I hid a smile.

"Can you tell us more about this guy who said he had to be at court?" Monkton leaned forward. "You said he was well spoken."

"Oh, he was. Not like me and Maizie. Or Warthog. Or one of the other fellas who was there. Mister Shifty I thought of him as. He had funny eyes."

Monkton made a note of that. "So, he wasn't necessarily ..." Monkton pulled a face. "Forgive me, he wasn't necessarily up in court on charges?"

"He wasn't necessarily a crook, you mean?" Hari wheezed in amusement. "Now that you come to mention it, no. I never thought of that! He might've been a beak or summink."

I glanced at Monkton admiringly. I hadn't caught that, but now that he'd raised it, that muddied the waters even more. A potential lawyer or judge mixing with a couple of former police officers and ordinary members of the public. It was hard to fathom a link between such disparate groups. Very much an us and them.

"No chance of this person being a carpenter?" I asked, just in case.

"Well, I s'pose he might've been. Anyfink's possible, ain't it? But 'e didn't strike me as the type. Soft 'ands and all that. Besides, I'd probably 'ave known him. You get to know others in the same trade don't ya? That's why I kind of know Maizie."

"She was a carpenter?" Monkton asked.

"No need to sound quite so astonished, best carpenter I ever knew—namely my ex-wife, she was a chippie—was a woman. But no, Maizie weren't no carpenter. She was like me, she was. A grass."

"A grass?" The realisation was like a bucket of cold water thrown from a height. I could hardly catch my breath. This was the link we needed.

"Yeah." Hari sneered. "A grass. A snitch. A police informant."

CHAPTER 13

"Well, well," said Monkton as we strolled back to the car. "I think we're finally getting somewhere."

"The attendees at this party were a mix of law and order and informants," I said, thinking of my own Snitch. Thank the goddess he hadn't received an invite.

"Subject to us identifying the rest of them, maybe." Monkton pulled his mobile out and began scanning his messages.

"Hari mentioned he had that wheat intolerance thingie," I mused.

"Coeliac disease," Monkton corrected me. "My brother has that."

"It means they can't eat wheat, right?"

"Yes."

"Well that's what I said. Wheat intolerance."

"But it's *more* than wheat. It's all gluten. Wheat, barley and rye and anything containing those."

"So no cake and sandwiches?" I asked. "Or pies and pasties? Crikey. I live on pies."

"No pasta, vinegar, soy sauce, Chinese food—"

"Ooh no. That's not for me."

"People don't choose to have coeliac disease, Liddell," Monkton said. "It can be quite nasty."

"No, sure." I rearranged my features to appear more sorrowful. "But Hari couldn't eat anything at the party, could he?"

Monkton nodded. "You're going back to the idea that there was some sort of poison in the food?"

"It seems reasonable," I said. "Apart from Hari still being ill."

"He said he drank some of the tea. Maybe that was contaminated to a lesser extent."

"Forensics haven't come back with anything yet?"

"Not so far. And neither has Mickey."

"It's a theory." I shrugged. "We will see what we will see, I suppose."

"Speaking of Mickey, I might head over and ask him what the latest is on our John Does. See if he has a name for Mister Shifty the beak. What are you going to do?"

"Have a conversation with Snitch," I said. "Seek some clarity about the person he witnessed leaving Fletcher Gate and find out what he knows about Hari and Maizie."

Monkton approved. "Sounds like a good plan. Do you need a lift? If you do, you'll have to wait for me to finish."

Mickey's lab was just down the road, hidden away from the rest of the hospital in a dark basement. After that, Monkton would be travelling from the hospital to Celestial Street, the back end of which was accessible for traffic. I weighed my options. I could walk through Witchycoo Park and get some air, which would be nice, then cut across the bottom of Celestial Street and through Cross Lane, or I could tag along while Monkton spoke to Mickey.

As much as I liked Mickey, Monkton didn't need a minder. "I'll check in with you later," I told him. "Thanks again for taking me to see Cerys."

"Let's touch base this evening?" Monkton suggested. "I'll call you."

"Okay." I smiled, waved and turned away, keen to make good time back to Tudor Lane. I walked quickly, in and out of the shade cast by carefully cultivated trees, through the busy hospital grounds, crossing the road and swinging through the iron gates into the park. So lost in thought was I, that I barely noticed the late summer blooms or the trees here bending under the weight of their foliage, but I did appreciate a moment to be out in the fresh air, away from hospitals and morgues or crammed alleys and smoky air.

So much had happened today, so much to think about. Was Cerys genuine? Would she give up the information she had? The link between the Labyrinthians and the tea party seemed to be growing. If Snitch could help me find—

"Psssssst!"

I slowed down, almost to a stop, glancing about, certain I'd heard someone hissing at me. There was no-one to be seen. *Must have been my imagination.*

"Psssst!"

I stopped. That hiss had originated a little behind me. Retracing my steps, I studied my surroundings. Trees. A bench. Flower beds—

"Elise! Down here!"

I dropped my gaze and there, among the white flowers —perfect camouflage for a fluffy white rabbit—was Minsk.

"Hey!" I moved closer, but she darted underneath the blooms.

"Are you incognito?" I asked.

"Preferably," she confirmed.

I skirted the flower bed, seating myself on the cleanest section of a weather-beaten bench, the wood slats coated with lichen and bird droppings. Once I'd made myself comfortable, I pulled my bag onto my lap and pretended to search inside it.

The flowers rustled gently as Minsk crept towards me. "Thanks," she said. "I don't want anyone to see us together."

"What's up?" I asked, settling on my mobile as the best way to deflect attention from myself and thumbing through my messages.

"I heard from a mutual friend."

"Okay." Assuming she meant Culpeper, I held the phone up to my ear. "Did he say where he was?"

"No."

"What's going on with him?" I asked. "Why the disappearance?"

"We didn't talk long, and he wasn't particularly forthcoming. Look, I told you about us—not my team, but the Dark Squad—investigating him," she whispered.

"For murder," I said, equally quietly, my eyes shifting left and right, keeping an eye on anyone who might be watching me.

"I couldn't say before, but it's some warlock from one of our older cases. He and our friend had a falling out a few years ago. He was found dead in an alley yesterday morning, and someone fingered our friend for it. When the top boss tried to speak to him, it turned out he'd disappeared and it didn't look like he'd been home."

I couldn't imagine Culpeper even had a home, let alone that he was in it very often.

"Did you ask him about the warlock?" I asked.

"Of course. He said it had nothing to do with him."

I supposed he would say that.

"He dismissed the whole thing out of hand," Minsk added. "He was more interested in any other rumours that were circulating concerning him."

"And are there any?"

"Yes. It's odd. There are a few. Different strands. A few alleging he can't be trusted. Bordering on saying he's corrupt. And there is talk that he was somehow behind everything that happened at your tea party."

"You're kidding me?"

"While my team haven't been fully briefed about the tea party murders—in fact, I'm not sure it's a Dark Squad case at all—there are whispers around HQ are that *our mutual friend* has gone rogue." Minsk huffed. "It's ridiculous. There's talk of an incognito Dark Squad team trying to track him down and bring him in!"

"Did you tell him this?"

"I did. He already had his suspicions. He said they were trying to blacken his name."

"Who's they?" I wanted to know.

Minsk shrugged. "He didn't stick around long enough to tell me that. He did suggest I ignore all the tittle-tattle though."

"And who is spreading the rumours?" I asked. "I mean, how can they possibly *know* that Culpeper did anything? DCI Wyld and I are on this full time at the moment, and we're no closer to knowing who did it. We're not even absolutely sure we know how it happened yet."

"That's just it." Minsk, hidden away in the undergrowth, sounded perplexed. "I've tried to find the source and failed. The Dark Squad is an elite force, not given to such pernicious muck spreading as other police forces—"

I giggled. "Cheers. We're not that bad."

"Oh, you get how it is, Elise. Ours isn't a comparable office environment full of administrators with nothing else to do but gossip all day." The flowers danced as she moved around. "How this stuff is being disseminated, I really can't tell, but you know, if you hear something enough, it's easy to start believing it."

"But Cul—sorry—our friend isn't one for worrying about such nonsense, is he? Why doesn't he just come back and put everyone straight?"

"You're assuming I had time for a long, drawn-out discussion, Elise." I heard a series of soft thumps, as though Minsk was battering the soil with her back legs. She certainly seemed fraught. "I didn't."

A niggle of uncertainty wormed its way into my brain. What if this was an elaborate ruse that Culpeper was using to cover his tracks? What if he was involved? Why run if he had nothing to hide? "Do you think he's done anything untoward?" I asked, carefully keeping my tone light.

"No." Minsk was adamant. "I'd put my life on it. He's a peculiar one, but he's straight as a die. Or as straight as anyone in the Dark Squad ever can be."

Interesting. I suppose when you were dealing with the blackest of the black, and the bleakest of bleak crimes, there had to be times when you engaged in subterfuge to get the job done. That's where the MOWPD differed—ostensibly—from the Dark Squad. The Dark Squad did whatever they needed to do to apprehend the bad guys. Whether what they needed to do was legal or not, that was a matter for them alone.

"But what I came to find you to tell you," Minsk said, interrupting my thoughts, "is that he wants to speak to you."

"He does?" I moved my phone away from my ear and stared at it as though this would somehow magick Culpeper on the line.

"He's not going to ring you, you dingbat," Minsk said.

"How—?"

"I don't know. He'll decide."

"When—?"

"When the time is right and it's safe to do so."

I frowned. "Safe? For him? Or for me?"

"For both of you, I would assume," Minsk replied, her voice tart. "Didn't someone try to kill the pair of you just forty-eight hours ago?"

I shifted uncomfortably on the hard wooden bench. A stronger breeze blew at the trees, the fresh fragrance promising rain. And soon. The leaves whispered as they danced and the light shimmied, casting fleeting shadows where previously there had been none. "When you put it like that ..."

"That's how *he* put it," Minsk told me. "Beware, Elise. You should have been one of those victims at the tea party, and just because you weren't, doesn't mean the perpetrator, or perpetrators, won't try again."

At some level I'd understood that, but denial, coupled with being so busy working on the case, had buried the danger in the subterranean layers of my subconscious.

"They want him, they want DCI Wyld, and make no mistake, they want you too!"

The harsh truth of Minsk's words followed me back into Tumble Town. Now every nook and cranny in every crooked, narrow lane held an unknown danger. My senses strained with every step I took, and I became newly alive to the whispers in the shadows and the faces behind dark windows. I kept my hand curled around my wand and controlled my breathing in order to listen all the better.

Feeling tense, I almost jumped out of my skin when my phone rang. It was Wootton.

"Hey," I said.

"Hi, boss. Just checking in," he said.

"Are you?" I narrowed my eyes suspiciously.

"Erm ... actually, Ezra wanted me to call and see if you were alright."

That would explain it. Ezra and his unerring sixth sense. "I'm fine," I said, more to convince myself than Wootton or Ezra. "But while I have you on the line, could you do me a favour?"

"Anything." That's what I liked to hear. Obsequiousness among the troops.

"See what you can find out about a Maisie Thistle-bristle."

"Maisie Thistlebristle," Wootton repeated, and I could picture him sitting at his neat desk, next to my slightly less organised one, writing down the name. "How are we spelling that?" he asked.

"I have no idea," I told him. "As it sounds, I would suggest."

"Rightio."

"Is Snitch there?" I asked.

"No. We haven't seen him yet. Do you want me to get in touch with him?"

"No. I'll do it," I said. "If I don't track him down I'll come back to the office."

"Okay, boss. See you later!"

I thumbed the screen to end the call and turned my face up. Had that been a spot of rain?

Gloom was already settling into Tumble Town. The gas lamps on their heavy iron brackets had been lit—not that anyone ever witnessed the lamplighters with their ladders, wick trimmers and oil out and about and doing their jobs— and in the quieter moments as I hurried along, I heard the unmistakable hiss of the gas and spit of the flame.

It reminded me of the fireplace at Fletcher Gate. That *had* happened. It hadn't simply been a figment of my over-tired imagination.

The first soft spots of rain fell on me, dotting my nose and cheeks. Large drops. I increased my pace, unwilling to face a soaking this close to the office.

Up ahead of me, a door opened on the right and a man stepped out into the alley. He wore a long black coat and a battered top hat. He didn't look at me, but from the angle of his head, I knew he was appraising me just as I was him. I slowed. He flipped the collar of his jacket up and tucked his chin down to his chest, all the better to hide his face.

Nothing unusual there.

He could have chosen to wait for me to pass—I'm not sure whether that would have made me more comfortable or not—but he didn't; he turned towards me and began to stroll down the lane.

I sidestepped into the first doorway, a slight step down, readying my wand in case he tried anything.

"You need eyes in the back of your head," someone whispered, so close to my ear I could have sworn they were standing with me.

"Don't mind him," said another voice. "He's not got you in his sights."

The man in the black coat walked past my waiting place, his eyes cast down but his senses reaching out, softly glancing mine, seeking confirmation I was harmless. I spotted dark hair curled behind his ears, the faintest of five o'clock shadows and bright blue eyes. Blue eyes were unusual among warlocks, for that's what I assumed he was. About my age. Satisfied, he never broke step, simply continued on his way.

There were female giggles in the shadows.

"She likes him."

"He's piqued her fancy!"

"I'm not surprised. He's 'aaaaaaandsome," drawled another voice.

"Pack it in," I growled, amused nonetheless. The rain was coming down harder now. I loitered where I was, in the dry, watching it. "Warlocks aren't my thing."

"No, you're a good girl," the first voice replied, undoubtedly mocking me, but only for the fun of it. These Shadow People I'd stumbled upon were playful. They cackled in response.

"A very good girl!"

"Who are you?" I asked, knowing there'd be no getting any sensible answer from them.

"I'm her."

"She's me."

I smiled. "Never mind."

If I made a run for it, I could be back at Wonderland in about five minutes. I'd be soaked, but perhaps not as soaked as if I walked. *Ha ha.* Or I could stay here and shoot the breeze with my amusing new friends.

"It's the others you have to watch out for." This was a new voice. Younger. No hint of amusement in her tone.

"Which others?" I asked, instantly on my guard.

"The ones who want to *hurt* you," she whispered.

"Who are they?"

"They're you." One of the original whisperers.

"You're them."

Darn it! They would frighten this new voice away. "Talk to me," I demanded. "The young one. Tell me what you know."

"She knows nothing." Now even the first whisperer had lost her playfulness. Her voice had turned hard.

The second whisperer sounded more melancholy. "She knows everything."

"Everything which is to be known."

"Which is nothing at all."

"Help me out," I begged.

"DC Liddell?" Snitch's familiar voice drifted out of the rain a few feet from me. "Is that you?"

"Snitch? Hi." I turned to him. He waited where he was, the rain lashing down on his hood. "Come under here." I grabbed his arm and pulled him under cover.

"I thought I heard your voice," he said, shaking himself like a dog. He smelt rather like one too.

"I was trying to talk to the people in the shadows."

"I don't suppose you was having much luck, DC Liddell," Snitch said. "They're never very helpful, I don't think."

"You shouldn't try to think," the first whisperer retorted. "It's a dangerous thing to do where you're concerned."

"Oh, I don't know, Maeve," another whisperer tittered. "He's a sensitive specimen. Still waters run deep and all that."

Snitch sniffed, snottily. I was tempted to rummage in my pocket for a tissue, but I had a feeling I didn't have any clean ones, and let's face it, Snitch was a grown man, not a boy. "You mind your business," he said.

"And leave the running to his friend," quipped the second whisperer.

More cackles.

They knew us. They knew enough about Snitch to make such remarks, and they knew I ran. Just how omnipresent were they?

"I was going to give you a ring when I got back to Wonderland," I told him. "I've had some—" I broke off, not sure how much information I wanted to share in the presence of our whispering friends.

"Was lucky I found you then, DC Liddell. I was off out to see Granny Gan Gan."

"Oh, sorry. If you want to go—"

"No, no. It's perfeckly fine. I'll visit her later."

"If you're sure?" I wasn't actually trying to persuade him otherwise, just making the right noises. He was on my payroll. I fully intended to put him to work.

"It's no problem, DC Liddell. Weren't important or nuffin."

I poked my head out from under the shelter of the doorway. From somewhere in the distance came a long, low rumbling grumble of thunder. "Looks like this is in for a while," I said. "We might as well go."

Snitch stuck his hand out to check on the weather, despite the fact the rain was now so heavy it was coming down in stair rods. "Owwww. It's still raining, DC Liddell."

"You're already wet through," I pointed out. "And I'll just have to live with it."

"Alright." Snitch shivered melodramatically. "*Where* are we going?" he wanted to know.

"Cockington Lane. You can talk to me as we walk."

Chapter 14

We didn't walk; we scurried—and we didn't talk; we just kept our heads down and moved as quickly as possible. Fortunately, Snitch knew a myriad of ways to get everywhere, and this afternoon he stuck to the slimmest passageways and narrowest alleys. You ran the risk of having to rub shoulders with various unmentionables, but the advantage was that you didn't get as wet because there was so little space between the terraces for the rain to squeeze through.

I slithered on the cobbles from time to time; they were greasy underfoot after a week or so with no rain and, at one stage, I almost tripped over an itinerant lying on his back in the gutter, a glass demijohn clasped tightly in his hand as though it was his most treasured possession ever. I guessed it might well be. But it would soon be an ex-treasured possession; only a couple of mouthfuls of yellow liquid remained inside it.

"Do you think he's alright?" I asked Snitch, who had thoughtfully waited for me.

Snitch nudged the guy with the toe of his boot. The man grunted. "He's alive, DC Liddell."

"That helps."

"He'll be fine." Snitch dismissed both the man and his condition out of hand and pressed on. I hurried after him.

Finally, hair pressed against my scalp and water seeping through every seam of my jacket, I recognised Cockington Lane. We paused to catch our breath at the top of the street —actually a crossroads—and regarded Wesley's Wigs from where we were.

Glancing around, I nodded at Snitch. "You wanted to tell me something yesterday before we found out about Dodo's book collection?"

"Yeeee-ah." Snitch wobbled his head from side to side. "To be honest it wasn't that useful, I don't think. I tried asking around, y'know, about people who were out and about the other night, right? I hung out in Corbett Lane and around The Burial Place, tried to dig up a bit of dirt and what have you ..."

I tried not to think of Snitch digging up bodies.

"But didn't come up with that much ..."

I interrupted him. "Do you think it was a man or a woman you saw?" I asked.

Snitch regarded me in surprise. "Erm ... I didn't pay it much mind, DC Liddell. It was a human."

"What do you think now?" I said.

Snitch looked most put out. "It was a chunky human, DC Liddell. A man, maybe?"

"Women can be chunky, Snitch," I reminded him.

"I suppose that's true. I hadn't really considered what flavour they was. Do you think the person I saw was a woman, then? That changes the whole sper-speck-tive, see, cos I thought I had a name for you."

A cold blob of water fell from above, hitting me right in the centre of my crown, startling me. "You came up with a name?" I asked, shaking my hair and spraying water around, much as Snitch had done earlier.

"I thought I had. A chap named Merlon Thistlebristle, lives on Corbett Lane, but when I asked folks, it turns out he had an alibi."

I shivered, partly with cold as the damp seeped into my bones, partly with anticipation. "Well now, isn't that a happy coincidence?"

Snitch regarded me quizzically. "Is it?"

"The woman I want to find is Maizie Thistlebristle. His wife, perhaps?"

"Could be." Snitch brightened. "That is, as you say, a happy coincidence, DC Liddell, but it's probably cos you're such an amazing detective!"

"Aw, shucks." I didn't mind basking in a little ill-placed hero-worship for a moment.

"DS Izax always said so."

"Did he?" That was nice.

"It's this way." Snitch pointed to his left, indicating a crooked lane that led around a bend and uphill. I followed him. "I mean, he said other not-quite-so-complimentary things as well," Snitch continued, "but least said soonest mended, I reckon."

Hmpf. Did he indeed? "I reckon too."

"Not far up here," Snitch called back, "then just off here to the right." We squeezed down a dingy passageway, as crooked as the lane. Whoever had built these houses had just thrown them on the ground higgledy-piggledy. They were squat two-storey buildings with sunken roofs, the eaves just about staying above the windows on the upper floor. These had to be some of the oldest buildings in Tumble Town, I imagined.

We didn't venture far. Snitch paused and indicated a door a little way ahead. "I spoke to this gentleman yesterday. He works at the Smash and Grab, in the warehouse. That's where he said this Merlon bloke was the other night."

By Smash and Grab, Snitch meant a cash and carry supermarket near Dead Man's Wharf. It had a poor reputation—mainly because it wasn't the most hygienic premises in Tumble Town and because the clientele couldn't control themselves. The manager had to employ security wizards, who sometimes roughed up the customers. But what could you expect when your clientele were witches, wizards, warlocks and other paranormal beings, many of whom lived on the breadline or in abject poverty and were desperate enough to borrow or steal, and sometimes use aggression too?

We stood quietly, observing the door for a few minutes. It amazed me that Snitch had succeeded in tracking the figure he had seen fleeing from Fletcher Gate down to this specific address. Alright, he hadn't managed to get the right person, but he was as close as dammit.

"I suppose we would need to verify his alibi," I said.

Snitch jumped in. "I snuck into the Smash and Grab office and checked the rota. He was definitely down to work that night, so that much is true, DC Liddell. Unfortunately,

I couldn't check the CCTV. Too many security guards about."

"I'm gobsmacked you managed to do that much!" I told him. He'd stolen into the supermarket's office? How very daring. I'm not sure I would have tried to do that. "You've saved me one job, at least."

My phone vibrated and I freed it from my pocket. "A message from Wootton," I said. "Oh, brill! Look at this." I turned the screen so Snitch could see. "Do you recognise this woman?"

Maizie—with a *Z* not an *S*, as it turned out—looked more than a little like Princess Fiona from Shrek in her troll form. Cute, chubby cheeks and a turned-up nose, although from what I could see of the side of her head, her ears were normal. Her hair was a bright red in this image. She'd be easy to identify. Funny that Hari hadn't noted that detail though.

"She does look vaguely familiar," Snitch said. He rapidly tapped his bottom lip, playing it like a keyboard using all the fingers on his left hand. "But why does she?"

"Hopefully it will come to you," I said, stuffing my phone in my pocket. "Right!" I flipped my soaking wet hair away from my face. "Let's see who's at home, shall we?"

Snitch, still playing piano on his mouth, traipsed after me as I made a beeline for our target. The front door of number 5 was grey. Perhaps it had once been white or pale blue or something a little more cheerful, but that had been a long time ago. Someone was at home; I could see a light burning at the window.

Fishing my credentials out of my chest pocket, I rapped confidently at the door. I sensed the area just inside become still. Someone squawked. At last there was a rustle from behind the door. Several bolts were turned or drawn back. A chain was released. Finally the door opened, just a crack, and a face—very much like the one I'd been sent by Wootton, but in this case a male version—stared out at me. "Can I help you?" he asked, almost solicitously.

Interesting. "Hi there!" I offered a business-like smile and opened my wallet to show my PI licence. "I'm DI Liddell. I was wondering whether I could speak to Maizie Thistlebristle?"

"What makes you think you'll find such a person here?" the man asked.

"I know this is her address," I told him. "I'd like to have a chat with her."

"I think you've been given the wrong information," the man informed me, not unpleasantly.

It was time to turn stern. I gave him a little deadeye. "Is it Mr Thistlebristle?" I asked. "Are you Maizie's husband? Because if you are, you need to know that I think her life is in danger."

His mouth dropped open.

"And, perhaps from a selfish point of view, not just her life but mine too!"

Mr Thistlebristle began to close the door. "And the life of my friend." I stuck my foot in the gap, thankful for my tough Dr Martens. "So one way or the other, I have to speak to her."

"Are you forcing your way in?" The man's endearingly chubby little face had started to redden.

"It's alright, Merle, it's alright." The man was pushed aside and Maizie—for it must have been she—appeared in his place. This Maizie didn't have red hair at all. She might once have done, but the colour had washed out, leaving it a multicoloured salt and pepper mix in desperate need of a trim. "He's my brother, not my husband."

"I apologise," I said, speaking calmly. "Maizie? May we come in? We *really* need to have a chat."

She pushed her head a little further out of the door. "There's two of you, is there? Oh." Her eyes narrowed when she spotted Snitch.

"Hi," Snitch said, and snuffle-laughed. "We have met before, haven't we?"

"Yeee-es." Maizie pursed her lips. "S'pose you'd best come in then."

We followed her into her small front room—the front door opened straight onto it—with Merlon scuttling ahead of us. "Put the kettle on, Merle," Maizie told him. "These two look like a pair of drowned rats."

"To be honest, I feel like one," I said.

"Let me grab a couple of towels."

"That's very kind of you—"

"Not that kind of me," Maizie retorted, "just don't want you dripping all over my best upholstery."

I glanced dubiously at the fabric on her three-piece suite, a worn brocade, but accepted the towel when she offered it to me, and clench dried my hair, wiped my face and dabbed at my clothes. Snitch did the same, then, after we took a seat, close together on the sofa, folded the towel over his knees like a blanket.

Maizie sat opposite us on one of the armchairs, clasping her hands in front of her chest. I noticed she was trembling.

Perhaps from cold, perhaps from anxiety. "You're here about the other night?"

"Yes," I replied softly.

"It didn't take you long to track me down."

"Track you down?" I asked. "What do you mean?"

"Are you here to arrest me?"

"Goodness, no!" I exclaimed. "I apologise if I didn't make myself clear. I'm a private investigator, but I was invited to that party. I was supposed to be there."

"You were one of the ones who were late?" Maizie's eyes shone with tears.

"Yes."

"Thank goodness. You're so lucky. You'll never know how lucky. It was ... the most awful thing I have ever seen in my life."

"I appreciate how narrow my escape was," I agreed.

Maizie began to wring her hands. "Have you come to arrest me? It wasn't me! I swear it wasn't me!"

"I know," I reassured her. "We've spoken to one of the other survivors—"

"Who survived?" Maizie's eyes bore into me.

"I probably shouldn't say too much at the moment." I smiled apologetically. "But perhaps that gives you a little comfort? That there were a few survivors?"

A tear trickled down Maizie's cheek. "But all those others ..." Her voice was a terrified whisper.

Merlon came in at that moment with two mugs of tea, one for me and one for Snitch. I'd have preferred coffee, but that didn't appear to be an option. "Would you like sugar?" he asked.

"Not for me, I'm fine." I wrapped my cold hands around the warm mug.

"I'll have six, please," Snitch replied, perfectly politely.

Ewww. Six! And that was Snitch being conservative, but when Merlon fetched a mug for Maizie and the sugar bowl for Snitch, I noticed the rascal took at least nine spoonfuls. No wonder he was missing his front teeth.

"What can you tell me about the other night?" I asked Maizie. "Why don't we start with your invite?"

"That was weird," Maizie told me. "At the time I didn't think it was, but it definitely was." She watched Snitch as he stirred his tea. "I work at the Lighthouse. It's a shelter for the homeless—"

"Owww, yeah. That's where I've seen you," Snitch recalled. "It's nice there."

A tiny light came on in Maizie's eyes. "Thank you. We work hard to make sure it's welcoming."

"You do a great job!" Snitch enthused.

"Vitally important," I added, although I didn't know the place personally.

"Thanks. I'm only a volunteer, but I do what I can."

"And the invitation?" I prompted her.

"One of our visitors pointed it out to me. Someone had pinned it on the noticeboard. But it had my name on it. They could have dropped it into the office."

"Do you still have it?" I asked.

She nodded, placed her mug on a coffee table and jumped up. She rifled through the pocket of a robe hanging on a hook by the door. "Here." She handed me the envelope. It had been rolled up and crumpled, but I smoothed it open and flattened the invitation as best I could.

"Tumble Town League of Charities," I read. "Dear Ms Thistlebristle. We are pleased to invite you to our prize-giving evening ... We have the honour of bestowing awards to noted members of our community who serve as volunteers in community settings, assisting those less privileged than others. We are thrilled to inform you that you have been nominated in the category of Caring for the Homeless and Dispossessed in recognition of your sterling work."

Huh. I sat back in my seat and once again admired the quality of the paper and the use of a coloured and embossed logo. Everything was impressively official. Whoever had set this up had gone to a lot of trouble to get it just right for every single person who had been invited.

"And you assumed this was genuine?" I asked.

Maizie threw herself down into her armchair. "I did. I had no reason to doubt it. I only began to worry when I recognised the copper."

"Tuttlewhirl?" I checked.

"Yeah." She grimaced. "Tuttlewhirl. Did he make it?"

I shook my head. "Sorry."

"Aiiiiiii." Her bottom lip wobbled. "You know, it almost seemed feasible that Tuttlewhirl would be there. I thought maybe he was on the board or something. You know, a dignitary, or what have you. But then I recognised one of the other wizards there ... don't know his name ... big bushy eyebrows ... and Wesley."

"You knew Wesley Warthog well?" I asked.

"Yeah, we knocked around together for some time. Just mates. Never nothing romantic, but I'd visit him from time to time, and I know he was working for old Tuttlewhirl as well ..."

"Ah." Hari had been right. "You were an informant for Detective Tuttlewhirl?"

Maizie shifted uncomfortably. "I don't class myself as an informant, but erm ... yeah, in a manner of speaking, I sometimes ... helped him out."

"And Wesley did too," I confirmed.

"No doubt in my mind. As soon as I saw him and Tuttlewhirl present I knew something wasn't right."

"Did any of the others mention that?"

"Yeah, one of the blokes ... posh, he was. Spoke like he had a plum in his mouth. He looked me up and down and said, 'I wasn't expecting to see someone like *you* here.' I mean, the out and out bloomin' cheek of 'im."

She rubbed her shoulders. "I wasn't comfortable, and I did consider doing a runner there and then, in fact I think I said so to Wesley, but he was interested in what was going on and he wanted a piece of cake, so he sat down, and then the others did. I tried to say we should wait."

"What caused you to leave?" I asked.

"I—" She leaned forward, running her hands through her hair, so that it stuck out in all directions. "I thought I saw something. It scared me." She fell silent.

"Can you describe it?" I asked.

"Urgh. You're going to think I'm crazy. Maybe I am. I've been doubting myself."

"Nothing you can say would make me think you were crazy," I promised. Not strictly true, but some thoughts we choose to keep to ourselves, right?

"I went out into the hallway. I wanted to check whether anyone else was coming, and in any case, as I said, I was already in two minds about staying or going ..."

The hallway. My ears pricked up.

"I glanced to my left and there was this other room there. The fire was blazing away, and it occurred to me that maybe other people had gone in there instead of joining us. You know. Maybe the party had split up." She shook her head. "But when I peered inside I saw a man. Tall. Thin. So ... pale." She shuddered. "And he was staring into the mirror."

I narrowed my eyes, saying nothing. I didn't want to lead my prime witness, after all. The person she was describing? That sounded an awful lot like Culpeper to me. And the fireplace? I just knew there was something off about it, no matter what Ezra had said.

"Or, at least, I thought he was staring, but suddenly, he threw his arm out." She demonstrated, showering the rug between us in tea but scarcely noticing. "He called out something—I don't know what it was—it was in a language I don't use. Then this mist—I don't know how else to describe it, started to flow from the mirror. Except I'm not sure it was a mist exactly because it oozed—" She stared at the wall, not seeing me and Snitch, unaware of her surroundings, thinking only of that moment. "Mists don't ooze, and this ... this thing ... it did." She clamped a hand to her mouth, creating a strangled sound. "Uh."

Merlon reached out to soothe her and she shot back in her chair and screamed, startling us all.

Snitch jumped a mile. "Owwwwwww!" he cried.

I clutched my heart. *Crikey.*

"For the goddess's sake, don't do that, Merle!" Maizie shrieked. "You know how jumpy I am!"

Merle backed away, recoiling in mock terror. "I'll get the biscuits, shall I?"

"Owww!" Snitch purred with pleasure, recovering quickly at the mention of his favourite treat.

Maizie met my eye and clamped her forehead between her palms. "This ooze began to slide out of the mirror and the pale, thin guy who conjured it started shouting." Merlon re-entered the living room clutching a dinner plate full of biscuits, moving around well within Maizie's eyeline and casting wary glances in her direction. It would have been comical, except that I was heavily invested in what she was telling me and I genuinely wanted to hear every detail.

"And then?" I demanded.

"And then I did a runner, love! What would you have done?"

Blast.

"I'd have done the same," Snitch said, helping himself to a couple of the biscuits that Merlon held out to him.

When I waved the plate away, Snitch took a couple more. "Just to be polite," he muttered.

"You said the man you saw in this room, he conjured the ... creature or ... ooze ... or whatever it was?"

"He did," Maizie replied stoutly, a defiant gleam in her eye. "Don't you believe me?"

"Of course I believe you," I said. I had no reason not to. She was an eyewitness, and every eyewitness is a valued resource. What she *thought* she saw and what *actually* happened might be two very different things though. There can be several different versions of an event, even if there is only ever one single truth.

We all have our own truths, but *the* truth is often the most intangible of beasts.

Especially for detectives.

Sipping my tea, I stared at her thoughtfully. "You didn't hear anyone else while you were in the library?"

"Library?"

"The side room," I corrected myself.

She shook her head, taking a moment. "Honestly, it all happened so fast and I wanted to get away."

I frowned. She wasn't being completely honest. She couldn't be. Snitch had told me he'd seen her exit after Monkton and I had entered the premises. We'd checked the library first and there had been no sign of anyone in there.

"I can see from your face that you don't believe me." Maizie sounded almost tearful now.

"Owww, we do," Snitch said. I sent a mental glare his way without actually turning my head. Perhaps he felt it because he leaned away from me. "Oww."

"You say you ran," I said. "Where?"

"Where?"

"Where?" Her voice had faded to a whisper and she had turned a little pale. She cast a nervous look at Merlon, and I noticed that he, still standing alongside Snitch and clutching the plate of biscuits, hunched his shoulders as though to defend himself.

"Yes," I repeated. "Where did you go?"

She sighed, a long, drawn-out plea for help. Finally, she blurted, "I went back into the dining room!"

I nodded, assuming she'd wanted to let the others know about what she'd seen, maybe warn them.

"I shouldn't have done it, I know I shouldn't have done it." She started to babble.

Merlon stepped closer to her. "Maize."

"No, no. I need to tell it all, Merle. I need to get it off my chest. It don't feel right. I shouldn't have done it!"

"Done what?" I asked, puzzled. Had she killed them after all?

"Maize. They'll arrest you."

"Owww!" Snitch, panicked, glanced around for the people who would arrest Maizie.

Tears slid down Maizie's nose. "I'd seen these candlesticks on the table and I really liked them." Her mouth turned down at the corners. "I went in there to grab a pair when the others weren't looking, and I intended to go out the back way—on a pretence, kind of thing—tell the others I wanted to find a bathroom or something." She drew in a shuddering breath.

"So even though you were scared of this thing that you'd seen in the libr— the side room, you still wanted to steal something?"

"A girl's gotta pay the bills!" Maizie returned sharply, and finally I saw a glimpse of her more authentic nature. Hard as nails.

She nodded at Merlon and, tutting, he abandoned the plate of biscuits beside Snitch and slunk back into the kitchen. I heard the distinct sound of rummaging in chaotic cupboards, the clanking of china and the clinking of cheap glass.

"Don't judge me," Maizie snarled as Merlon returned with the candlesticks. I recognised them. They matched the ones that had been arranged on the table and the mantel-piece. I hadn't noticed that two were missing.

"Oww, I completely understand," Snitch said, nibbling on a Jammie Dodger.

"Did you warn them?" I asked, because burglary was one thing, but aiding and abetting an offender was something entirely different.

Maizie's face was the colour of ash now, the defiant glint in her eye still fiery but almost with a fever.

"It was too late," she told me, her voice flat. "They were all collapsed." She swallowed. "I would have called the police, but then I heard someone at the front door." She caught her breath, remembering. "I was petrified. There's some creature in the side room. Dead people all around me. I grabbed the candlesticks and tried to find my way out the back through the kitchen, but the door was locked and the windows were barred so I couldn't go anywhere."

She wiped her eyes with a shaking hand. "I ran back through the dining room. One of them fell off his chair right at my feet. I slowly opened the door into the hallway and it was clear. I just scarpered. Ran out and kept going until I got home."

I nodded and sat back.

This version of events I could believe.

"Are you going to arrest me now?" Maizie demanded.

"No," I said, not that I had the official capacity to do so anyway. "I'm not sure that would be in the public interest."

She sank back in her seat. Merlon inhaled deeply, similarly relieved. "You can have the candlesticks back," he said.

"I'll take them because you never know what evidence

might be found on them," I agreed. "But!" I lifted a finger. "And this is a serious but—"

Maizie's upper teeth caught at her lower lip. "What?"

"I think you need to go into hiding."

Maizie shot a look at her brother.

"Both of you," I added. You could never be too careful.

Merlon cringed. "Why?" he asked.

"Whoever killed those poor people at the tea party tried to get everyone together in one room," I explained. "Humans being what they are—busy, running late, curious —" *Tardy, thieves*, I wanted to add. "—they didn't manage it."

"You think whoever killed all those others still wants me?"

And me. And Monkton. "Yes." I told her straight.

"How come?"

"That's what we need to figure out next," I told her.

CHAPTER 15

"I need you to stand on lookout for me," I told Snitch. We were standing outside Wesley Warthog's shop. I peered inside the window, examining the shadows. Perfectly dark inside. The police presence had now been recalled, although the crime scene tape was still attached to the front door. That would please the neighbours. Both shops on either side of Wesley's Wigs were open. Or, at the very least, the lights were on. They weren't doing any business.

Nothing could be more off-putting to potential customers than crime scene tape, surely? Particularly in Tumble Town, where the last thing anyone wanted was to have the police snooping around.

"Rightio, DC Liddell." Snitch shrugged, slowly swivelling his eyes left and right.

"Sorry about the rain," I said, running my finger lightly along the slither of a gap where the door met the jamb.

"I can't really blame you for that, can I?" Snitch snuffle-laughed. "It's in for the foreseeable, according to Granny Gan Gan."

"Is that right?" I tapped the wood at the top where I'd expect to find a bolt. There was one. Something simple. It slid back easily.

"Oh yeah, she consults her oracle. It tells 'er what she needs to know."

"What does she need to know?" I asked, crouching down to search for a lock on the bottom of the door and making conversation for conversation's sake, feeling guilty for dragging Snitch around in such foul weather. Although, to be fair, he did have his uses and I was paying him.

"Well, the weather, obvs. Always helps to know whether to wear wellies or whatnot. And how much to bet on the gee-gees."

"Gee-gees?"

"Horsies," Snitch told me, his tone a study in patience.

"I know what gee-gees are, Snitch," I told him. The bottom lock slid beautifully across. "I meant, so she likes to bet on the horses, does she?"

"She does. She never wins nowt though. It's all a bit pointless if you ask me. Not that she ever does. If I had that kind of money I wouldn't waste it on a bunch of three-legged nags with croup."

I chuckled. "And what would you do with that kind of money?" The middle lock was going to prove trickier.

"I'd open a little electrical store," Snitch told me. "Bartholomew Aloysius Rich," he said, carefully recounting his full name, a name that nobody ever used. "Electronics Bought and Sold."

"*Snitch's Fix Its* has a ring to it," I said, grimacing as the lock I was trying to magickly entice open stubbornly refused to budge.

"S'not partickerly sophistimicated though, is it, DC Liddell?"

I heard the faint reproach. "No, you're right," I said. "Electronics bought and sold"—and fenced, no doubt—"has much more of a ring to it."

Clunk.

"Got it!"

I pushed the door open. That chemically fragrance of cheap plastic hit me straight away. I wondered again whether the room had been magickly cleansed. If it had, it would carry the same faint tang. There was a fusty warmth to the shop too. No surprise, given that it had been closed up for the best part of twenty-four hours. A muted light filtered through the dirty windows, and dust motes twirled in front of me. I reached into my pocket, pulled out my phone and used the light from the torch to illuminate matters further.

"Do you want me to stay out here, DC Liddell?" Snitch queried.

"No," I decided. "You might as well come in."

I moved further inside, giving him room, and he followed me. We dripped with every step.

"Quiet, innit?" Snitch stared around at the hats. "It's like a dressing-up shop." He reached for a top hat. "Not as nice as Hattie's, are they?"

"No, you're right, not the same quality." I watched him fiddle with the hat, checking the label, then donning it. He didn't have the face for hats at all.

"I wouldn't waste your money," I told him, and headed for the counter. I wanted to take a closer look at what I'd seen there, the catalogues and things.

"Don't I suit it?" Snitch asked. "I always imagined I'd look quite dapper in a top hat. When I have my electronics shop, I shall buy one from Hattie, and I shall stand in the doorway and greet my customers. Good day to you, Wizard Heartbreak. Good evening, Witch Crowkind." He bowed.

"Look in the mirror," I said, pulling out the pile of catalogues.

"Which mirror?"

I glanced up, meaning to direct him to one while throwing in a bit of a tsk-tsk and a wry shake of the head, but to my surprise, I couldn't immediately see one.

I turned, expecting there to be one behind the counter, but there wasn't. Puzzled, I went through to the small back room. Perhaps there was a dressing room? No.

In fact, there wasn't a single mirror on the whole ground floor. Nothing fixed to the walls. Nothing portable.

Why would a hat seller not have a mirror?

Or, as I'd noticed earlier, much in the way of stock?

Unless his primary business was nothing to do with selling hats.

Unless the hat shop was just a cover for something else that he did.

Like fence goods? Perhaps he fenced items that Maizie stole. Maybe ... just maybe, she and Merlon had a good thing going on at the Smash and Grab, and they were stealing stuff and bringing it to Warthog, who would sell it below the counter. For a cut, of course.

"You've got that look, DC Liddell." Snitch interrupted my thinking.

"What look?" I asked.

"The look you get when you're just about to send someone down forever."

I shook my head. "I don't do that anymore. I'm just an investigator."

"Well, you've got the look of someone who's about to murder someone, then."

"Ha!" I returned to the counter, leaving Snitch to delude himself about how much his top hat suited him without providing evidence to the contrary, and pulled the catalogues out. I'd flicked through the pile earlier, studying the covers without reaching the contents. I couldn't imagine that *British Hat Wholesale*, *House of Hair* or even *Fantasy Fez and Fedoras 2U* would help me much, and I'd assumed the police who had searched the premises earlier would have properly shaken everything down looking for loose notes or letters.

But halfway down the pile, as I prepared to flip through *Kerlinkity's Konical Bonnets*, the catalogue fell open where the spine had been broken and I realised I was looking at an A4-sized slim notebook using the catalogue outer as its binding. The notebook had been formatted in the style of a ledger, with hand-ruled lines and headings. There were several columns. Date. From. Payment. Information. The handwriting was tiny but neat. If I squinted and used the light of my phone, I could just about read it.

In almost every case, the 'from' name listed 'Tuttle'.

The payment was something small and insignificant. Usually a tenner. Sometimes twenty pounds. I spotted three or four fifty pounds. Naturally, it was those I was most interested in.

13th May 2009, read the first one. *Tuttle. £50. Rynth.*

Rynth?

The hairs on the back of my neck prickled. *Labyrinthians*?

I flicked through the pages, finding the next fifty-pound entry. *26ᵗʰ September 2010. Tuttle. £50. Taurus.*

Taurus!

The names alternated. *Rynth. Taurus*. Others that I didn't know. *Gemini. Capricorn*. And back to *Rynth*.

And there again. March 2011. January 2012. Three in August. 2013. 2014. None in 2015 or 2016. I flipped the pages more slowly. There! Two in 2017. Three in 2018. Half a dozen the following year. One in 2020. Four in 2021. And on …

The final entry had been four days ago. And the payment had been two hundred pounds.

Two hundred!

For information about a 'pool of tears'.

That's what it said. Pool of Tears. Using capital letters.

"Snitch?" I called. He was now trying on a beret. He looked like a little French witch boy.

He threw the hat away and hurried over to me. "Yes, DC Liddell?"

"Have you heard of The Pool of Tears or a pool of tears?"

He knitted his eyebrows together. "I don't think so, DC Liddell. Is it a swimming pool for stressed people?"

What? "I have no idea."

"A pub, maybe?" He sounded doubtful.

"Could be." I tucked the book under my arm. Removing it wouldn't be strictly protocol, but I could scan the pages and then return the original, and no-one would be any the wiser. "I'll get Wootton to run a search," I said. Right after I'd made him scan this book for me.

Thump.

Snitch and I simultaneously tipped our heads back, scanning the ceiling.

Something upstairs.

"Owww," Snitch groaned, but quietly. "Should we leave?"

"Tempting," I said and pulled out my wand. I had no intention of leaving.

Snitch pulled a face. "DC Lidd—"

"You can wait outside if you like," I whispered, gesturing at the shop door. "Hide. I'll join you in a minute."

"Owwww." Snitch began to creep backwards. "If you're not blown to smithereens or something ..." he muttered.

Ignoring him, I tiptoed through to the small room at the back. The stairs to the second floor were here through a narrow door cut into the wall. I remembered from yesterday that there had been no carpet on the wooden floorboards. There was little hope of me making it upstairs without being heard.

Always assuming someone was up there, of course. For all I knew, there was a recalcitrant pigeon trapped in one of the small bedrooms. I stared upwards as a floorboard creaked almost directly above my head.

Not a pigeon.

Unless it was wearing work boots.

I pulled open the door, craned my head around and stared up into the void. The stairway was dark, but a little light streamed in from the windows and pooled on the landing at the top.

Footsteps.

Clump. Clump. Clump. Clump.

Walking from the rear.

I took the first stair, eyes straining, wand held aloft.

Clump. Clump. Clump.

Into the front bedroom.

Clenching my jaw, I climbed the next few as quietly as I could. Heel and toe down at the same time. Softly. Softly.

Clump. Clump. Clump. Clump. Clump.

They'd walked through to the back room. What were they doing?

I shifted my weight. Carefully mounted the next two steps.

The stair creaked.

The mood changed. The atmosphere crackled. So finely tuned was I, straining to see and hear, I could make out tiny sparks of energy glowing orange in the air around me, drifting like gentle embers.

Clump-clump-clump-clump-clump-clump-clump—

Someone raced from the rear to the front bedroom.

I shot up the next few steps, ducked and twisted, hoping to catch sight of them as they sped past me.

A blur. Little more than a shadow. I had the sense of thin limbs. Wings. It streaked past me, leaping into the air as it crossed the threshold. I went after it, but as I ran into the room, the double-panelled window burst open and the thing—whatever it was—leapt out into the darkness.

I chased after it, as slow as a snail by comparison, finally slamming into the wall and reaching out to grab onto the windowsill to prevent my momentum from propelling me forwards. Gravity could be the harshest of mistresses. Panting, I gazed down into the street. Something black—small, no larger than a cat—lay on the cobbles.

Snitch edged out of a doorway across the road and leaned down to pick up whatever it was.

"Is that all it was, DC Liddell?" he called, holding the object aloft. Its neck hung at a perverse angle.

A carrion crow.

"Lucky for us," Snitch said, and cradled the creature in his arms. "Not so lucky for you, sweet bird," he crooned.

Shaking my head, I pulled the windows closed. It hadn't been a crow. No way. It had reminded me of the robed spirit figures I'd first stumbled across when tracking Dodo's murderer down, before my detective agency had become a thing.

As I latched the windows, I noticed something written in the grime. I tilted my head to get a better look.

Your next, it said.

I frowned. The misspelling annoyed me as much as the sentiment. And okay, this didn't have to mean anything; just kids messing around. Even one of the junior police officers. Hell, I'd known detectives pull pranks like this.

Except, when I scraped at the window with the pad of my index finger, I realised that this particular little love note had been written on the outside of the glass.

That would suggest a level of imagination and dedication to the cause that I doubted many of my colleagues possessed.

"Great," I whispered. Unease gnawed gently away at my innards. "That's just super-duper."

As I turned away, my boots crunched on glass. Not from the window. The glass in those remained intact. Peering down, I noticed my face reflected back at me a dozen or so times.

Pieces of a mirror.

Given that there was nothing else in Warthog's living quarters—no furniture, clothes, books or other belongings —I found that odd. Had someone broken in here just to steal or smash a mirror?

Bizarre.

Crouching down, I pulled the larger pieces together to form a rough rectangle. My face, fractured and scarred, stared back at me in wonder. I couldn't see anything interesting about the mirror. Nothing unusual.

Shrugging, I began to stand, but suddenly the image swirled and distorted. My stomach heaved as my head swam. Vertigo. I swallowed hard, gazing into the mirror, trying to interpret what I was seeing. Arches? Victorian brickwork. A thin face lurched into view. As pale as death. Eyes ringed in black.

"DS Culpeper!" I whispered. "Where are you?"

"You're in danger," he said, and his voice crackled and hissed, as though he were being tuned in and out on an old-fashioned wireless. "You're in danger. And I'm in danger. We all are. Find me, DI Liddell."

His voice faded away.

"Where are you?" I cried.

But the image had disappeared and, once again, I was staring at my own face. A study in concern.

CHAPTER 16

"Maizie Thistlebristle was an informant for Tuttlewhirl," I recapped for Monkton and my team in the Wonderland office much later that day, drawing a line on the badly marked whiteboard Wootton had erected on an old easel. It wobbled every time I put any weight against it, but for now, it was all I had. After nearly two hours with the Thistlebristles in an attempt to garner more information from them, Maizie had disappointed me by keeping some details very close to her chest.

In addition to being less than forthcoming, she'd refused point-blank to move out of her house and go into hiding.

"This is our life," she'd insisted. "Besides, if they wanted me dead, they'd have come after me already. They know where I work, don't they?" And I'd had to agree with her.

If I expected anyone in the room to be interested in what I was saying, I was sadly deluded. Wootton slumped in his chair—he'd had a long day, bless him. Dodo and Ezra were at their respective desks, Ezra with his feet up and a trilby pulled low over his forehead, while the wizard doodled absently on a pad. Monkton, all shades of exhausted, was slouched on a comfy seat and looked ready to bed down for the night right where he sat.

Then there was Minsk. She stared out of the window into the darkness beyond, but not really seeing anything—certainly not the derelict factory building opposite. I'd been surprised when she turned up, completely unannounced. I could smell the night air on her damp fur. A cool mist had enveloped Tumble Town this evening, brought on by the wet conditions and falling temperature. It carried with it the scent of the Thames, a slight salty tanginess mixed with diesel and industrial chemicals, and wrapped itself around the buildings in Tudor Lane, masking them with thin fingers while effectively deadening noise. An army could have marched over the cobblestones below us, and we wouldn't have heard them.

Having said that, the hammering of boots on the creaking stairs might have been a giveaway, and in any case, Hattie had retired to bed, and she'd have been the first person to come out and complain had anyone interrupted her beauty sleep.

Vociferously.

Yep. She'd make an effective early warning system if anyone was intending to cause us trouble tonight.

"We know Wesley Warthog was an informant, too." I drew another line. "And Hornswoggler. Meanwhile—" I changed to a red marker. "Tuttlewhirl, both myself and DCI Wyld, plus two others that we know about, were serving or former MOWPD." The 'two others' referred to Culpeper and Ibeus, of course. Ibeus had never been ejected from the force because she'd disappeared with a warrant out for her arrest. She'd have faced the consequences had she been charged, but for the time being, she had merely been suspended in her absence.

Monkton had cautioned me against sharing too much information about either Culpeper or Ibeus. Ibeus had become known as victim J Doe—as she was the only dead female—while Culpeper was identified only as *C*. "We also know of a magistrate in attendance, Fusty Dankcellar."

"Oh, yeah!" Monkton rolled a stiff shoulder. "We have another name—Wizard Megrin Folstrop."

"What do you know about him?" I asked.

"A special constable in his younger years. He ran the Grim and Gory Whippersnappers' Club on Belfast Lane—"

"I was a member of them for a while!" Snitch piped up from where he was sitting cross-legged on the floor beside Dodo. He had another of those electrical contraptions with him that he liked to pull apart and put back together. I had no idea what they were. Initially I'd assumed they were phones, and maybe, once upon a time, they had been, but more recently these things were more matchbox sized and packed full of tiddly circuit boards and minuscule screws. "I remember Wizard Folstrop! I didn't know 'e was ex-police."

"It was a long time ago," Monkton reiterated.

"What are the Gory Whipperwotsits?" I asked.

"They're a bit like the Boys' Brigade," Monkton told me and stifled a yawn.

"Boys' Brigade?" Snitch asked. "Beggin' your pardon, I

finks they're more scouts, kind of. They make things. Magick things. And study dead stuff."

"Sounds great," I said. This is what the kids of Tumble Town got up to, was it? No wonder they all grew up to be mad, bad and dangerous.

"In any case, he's another victim who had been in the force," Monkton continued. "He had good community contacts."

"Why did he leave?" I asked.

Monkton glared at me, then tutted. He hadn't thought to check. "I'll look into it," he said.

I added Folstrop to my whiteboard list of doom and jabbed the pen towards Monkton. "In my view, that's strong evidence that all of our victims were put together in that room because of what they had in common—"

"What did they have in common?" Minsk asked, turning her head to gaze at me. I'd never seen a rabbit look tired before, but even she had shadows under her eyes. I wanted to pick her up and hug her. "Definitively," she added, with a tone so sharp it could have sliced through a diamond without leaving a whisper of residue. I parked the idea of giving her a hug, deciding a stiff drink might be more up her street.

"Taurus," I said. "The Labyrinthians."

Silence.

Monkton blew out a silent breath and shook his head.

"It's the only logical explanation," I continued. Nobody else punched the air in joy or even brightened just a shade. There was only cold, hard, tired silence. We were all done in. We had nothing concrete as proof.

"Think about it." I carried on undeterred. "Monkton,

me, Ibeus, Warthog ... we've all had undertakings with the Labyrinthians. Tuttlewhirl too, by the looks of it. And I'd lay good money on Maizie and Hornswoggler selling information about Taurus or some other Labyrinthian bigwig to Tuttlewhirl."

"Will they admit to that?" Minsk asked, hell-bent on finding proof.

"I doubt it." Monkton sighed.

"Maizie definitely won't. She thinks she's safe as long as she doesn't rock the boat. She wants to save her skin. That's pretty much all she's thinking about. She claimed that all the information she passed on was harmless. She told me some of it wasn't even true, just a way to make a fast buck."

"Having seen those records you misappropriated—" Monkton said.

"I'll put them back," I reminded him.

"I'd say Tuttlewhirl was fully aware of the value of snippets that were passed on to him," he continued. "A tenner really isn't much."

"Cor," whispered Snitch, with an edge of indignation.

"In this instance I'd agree," Ezra chipped in. "I'd pay ten minimum for not much. I expected some of my informants to try it on with me. They'd give me information that was already common knowledge or try and pass on gossip or something entirely meaningless. Occasionally there would be something in the gossip that was worth paying attention to, but more often than not, all I was doing was providing funds for a beer and a takeaway in return for a load of hot air."

"Therefore, can we assume there must have been value in Tuttlewhirl's payouts of twenty and fifty?" I asked.

"I think that's likely," Ezra confirmed. "Never mind the two hundred. Now *that* is a lot of money."

"It seems that Tuttlewhirl paid Warthog two hundred pounds for information about a pool of tears," I said. "Or 'The Pool of Tears'. Wootton's going to research that for me in the morning." I smiled at my office manager, and he sat up a little straighter.

"Tomorrow?" he asked hopefully. "You mean we *will* be going home sooner or later?"

"I'll see if I can swing that," I said.

Wizard Dodo grunted. I eyed him suspiciously. "Something to add?" I asked him.

"The boy won't find it," he said, dismissing us.

Wootton pouted. "My research skills may be amateur in comparison to yours, but they're getting better."

"Don't put yourself down," I said. "I'm perfectly happy with the work you do, and"—I shot a dirty look Dodo's way—"I pay you; ergo, I'm the only person you need to impress."

"Ner!" Wootton poked his tongue out at Wizard Crotchety Pants.

Dodo rolled his eyes. "What I mean to say is that the boy won't find anything out because it doesn't exist." His head swivelled, eyes bright, taking in the rest of us. We all stared back at him with something akin to rapt attention, although it might just have been numb exhaustion. "The Pool of Tears is a mythical place. Nobody knows where it is or what it is."

Minsk perked up and hopped to the end of Wootton's desk. "Tell us about the myth."

"It's a strange one, I must admit." Dodo clicked his

fingers and a long curly pipe appeared from nowhere. Settling back in his chair, he puffed away on it for a moment. The tip burned red. He inhaled deeply, then blew a series of perfect smoke rings.

Snitch stared up at him, a picture of total devotion. "Cor."

"The Pool of Tears was first referenced by monks in the fourteenth century. They spoke of a darkness. A place without structure, where time was fluid. The records were scant, as you might expect from that time, but there was some insinuation that people had visited it." He puffed away on his pipe, watching our reactions. "It was all written in Latin, of course."

I fought to curb my impatience. "And had they? Visited it?"

Dodo shrugged. "Impossible to tell. There are no other written accounts, but we are talking about a time when very few people could read and write. Anecdotes were handed down, generation by generation, and it appears The Pool of Tears simply faded into obscurity."

"But?" Minsk asked, thumping her back leg, as impatient to get to the point as me.

Dodo gestured with his pipe. I could almost smell the sweet appley scent of his ghost tobacco. "You're a sharp one, you are." He nodded. "Yes, there is a but. We might never have known anything else about it except that there was fresh speculation about such a place, way back in the 1880s. Some streetwalker ..." He tipped his head back, searching the rafters. "What was her name? Smiley? Smiler? No! She was called Lyla. Lyla Worstead. A streetwalker. She went to the police and swore blind that she and a gentleman client she spent time with, can't remember his name, went through a portal to The Pool of Tears. The gentleman never came out again, according to her statement."

"So what did she say The Pool of Tears was?" I asked.

The old wizard turned his mouth down at the corners. "No-one ever asked her and no-one ever found out. The chap's body was recovered from the river and she was charged with murder."

"And that's it?" I slapped my desk. "How frustrating!"

"No-one pursued The Pool of Tears lead?" Ezra asked, ever the detective. "I would have done."

"I have no idea. I can only tell you what the records say." Wizard Dodo shrugged. "Perhaps someone did investigate but it didn't lead anywhere and they didn't write it up. Seemed an open and shut case at the time, I think. The woman was obviously crackers." He held his pipe up before Ezra could butt in again. "What *is* interesting is that several academics have written studies about The Pool of Tears, and the best they can come up with is that it isn't a place so much as a state of mind, brought on by opioid abuse or some such. Lyla, for example, was a known addict. There were dozens and dozens of opium dens in Tumble Town back then."

"And that's it?" I asked, disappointed. "It doesn't exist?"

"I'm not saying that, oh office-usurper-of-my-recent-acquaintance." Dodo arched an eyebrow. "Not at all, but I am saying that no-one has ever found any physical trace of it, and there is nothing—" He pointed at Wootton. "Nothing at all—in the records to say otherwise."

I slumped over my desk, head in my hands. All leads were going in the same direction. Nowhere.

Minsk jumped down from Wootton's desk. "I need to go," she announced.

I looked up. Her appearance in the office this evening had been a surprise, and now, abruptly, she wanted to leave again.

"Walk me down," she told me and, without saying goodbye to anyone else, hopped away.

Pushing my chair back, I said to Wootton, "Why don't you pack up? I'll see you and Snitch tomorrow."

"Thanks, boss." Wootton began to shut his computer down.

I traipsed after Minsk, navigating the stairs by the subdued illumination of a couple of low wattage wall lights and taking great care to tread quietly so as not to wake up Hattie, slumbering in her flat on the middle floor.

Once down on Tudor Lane, I instantly regretted not bringing my jacket, although to be fair, it was still soaked through from my earlier misadventures. The mist was thick, and the drizzle relentless. I wrapped my arms around myself and peered into the gloom seeking Minsk. When I couldn't immediately find her, I walked down the lane a little, away from The Hat and Dashery and towards The Pig and Pepper.

Up ahead the mist was yellow, reflecting the light that spilled out from the pub's open door. Business was brisk this evening, judging by the plinkity plonk of some old piano and the raucous singing of *Daisy, Daisy* from inside. I checked my watch. Not long till the bell rang for last orders.

"Pssst!" Minsk stepped out of a doorway. "Here."

I slithered over the cobblestones and joined her. "What's up?" I asked. "You seem on edge."

"I am on edge!" She craned her neck back to glare at me. I crouched to make it a little easier for her to be angry with me or the world or whatever it was that was occupying her mind.

"You're concerned about Maizie's story about the man and the mirror, aren't you?" I'd briefly recounted the facts without mentioning names. I was kind of beholden to do so seeing as Snitch had been there too. I could see Minsk had jumped to the same conclusion I had.

"That Thistlebristle woman ought to be brought in for questioning," Minsk retorted.

"I thought the same," I replied, "but DCI Wyld wasn't so keen." I lowered my voice to a barely audible whisper. "If the inference is that Culpeper conjured that thing, whatever it was, then isn't that tantamount to saying it was him who killed all those people at the tea party?"

Minsk performed an angry hopping dance. "I could tear her story apart—"

"I really don't think that's a good idea," I warned the irate rabbit.

"I could produce a digital line-up!"

"Of tall, pale men," I agreed. "I know."

"There are thousands of men in Tumble Town alone who would fit that description," Minsk insisted.

I somehow doubted that. Culpeper looked like no-one else I had ever come across, but I decided not to argue. Proving Culpeper's innocence was evidently a hill Minsk was prepared to die on.

"I saw him," I blurted out. I'd kept the strange encounter in Wesley's Wigs to myself until now, unsure what it contributed to our investigation.

"You did?"

"In a broken mirror, of all things."

"What did he say?"

"He didn't say much," I replied. "Just warned me that I was in danger. I already knew that."

"Where was he?"

"I couldn't tell," I admitted. "It looked like every other place I know in Tumble Town. It was dark. There were arches."

"That's not much to go on," Minsk grumbled.

"I know. Maybe he'll reach out to me again." I'd just have to keep looking in mirrors, I supposed.

"He didn't say anything about the murders?"

"No."

Minsk huffed in fury. "We must exonerate him!"

"We will. And I want to support you," I said, "but I have to keep an open mind. You know that."

"I understand," Minsk said, but her eyes gleamed with a fiery wrath.

I sighed. "For what it's worth, I can't see Culpeper being behind this. I *can* see him being a target for—"

"It's not ssssafe."

"Not safe!"

Whispering around us. Minsk and I locked eyes, and I automatically reached for the pocket where I kept my wand.

Except I wasn't wearing my jacket.

"Not safe."

Quiet footsteps travelled towards us. I stood and stepped in front of Minsk. Whoever was coming our way didn't need to know of her existence.

Pad. Pad. Pad.

Soft shoes in this weather.

I twisted sideways, keeping Minsk behind me and angling my neck to peep out. A man in brown robes, the hood pulled up, his chin tucked down so I couldn't see his face. His feet, flicking out from beneath the robes as he hurried our way, sported leather thong sandals.

He might have seemed innocent enough on any other night, but it had been a tense few days. I relaxed my knees, wiggled my fingers, prepared to lash out if he made any move that I deemed suspicious.

He held his head at a downward tilt, although I sensed he was aware of me standing there. His hands were hidden in the folds of the robe, and he neither slowed his pace nor sped up.

It seemed at first as though he would continue past us. He drew level and his head lifted perhaps an inch. I couldn't see a hint of his features, but later I would recall an image of two pinpricks of burning light where his eyes should have been.

In moments of intense danger, two things happen. One, everything speeds up. Two, everything slows down. I can't explain that. Time bends. What happened next was over in less than a handful of seconds, and yet I can remember every detail as though there was a beat of time between each thought, reaction, emotion ...

His head swivelled. Just a fraction. An arm fought to free itself. My thinking sped up. *He's not walking past. He's intending to harm me. No time to hesitate. Hit him with a defensive blast—*

But even as I thought those things, he was crumpling towards the pavement, followed, what felt like an aeon later but had to have been virtually simultaneous, by a loud snap of explosive energy. He sagged, his legs giving way, but at the final second, when he should have smacked down on the cobblestones, everything changed. Skeletal black wings —smoky yet silky and far less dense than the suffocating mist all around us—unfurled. Creaking, cracking, membranes snapping ...

Then ... *Phwoomp! Phwoomp!*

Two flaps of those hideous appendages and the thing flew high above The Pig and Pepper to be swiftly lost from sight.

Only his robes remained but, as I turned to examine them, they burst into bright white flames, burning furiously for a couple of seconds before evaporating completely away, leaving little more than a fistful of burnt embers sizzling in the rain.

I gazed down. Minsk, her head poking out between my feet, one paw still held out, aiming at where the man had been walking, sneezed.

"That took care of him," she said.

I'd been too slow to react and I knew it. I breathed out, partly in relief, partly in annoyance.

"I've seen his type before," I said. "When I was investigating Dodo's murder. One of them met up with Cerys."

"And we know she was working for the Labyrinthians—"

"Don't say it, don't say it!" something whispered, and the call was taken up.

"Don't say it, don't call them!"

"Don't call them forth."

I shrugged them off, these strange Shadow People, who heard everything and were absolutely no help to anyone.

"Unless Culpeper is working with them—"

Minsk stamped her paw. "Of course he isn't!"

"Then he has nothing to worry about." The whole Culpeper thing was irritating. Didn't we have enough on our plates without having to worry about his whereabouts? Chances were, he had evidence that would help our enquiry. "He just needs to stop playing silly beggars and come forwards." I jerked upright. "Oh!"

"Oh?" Minsk asked, craning her head to look up at me.

"What if he can't? What if they've got him? He told me he was in danger. He asked me to find him."

"Hell's bells, Elise," Minsk hissed. "Then we've a missing person's case to worry about as well as multiple homicides!"

CHAPTER 17

"You didn't need to chaperone me," I scolded Ezra as we arrived back at the office the following morning. Having tossed and turned all night long, I'd woken with the dawn and chosen to forsake my usual morning run. I'd taken my seat in the window, cradling what I assumed would be the first of the many coffees I would need to get me through the day while staring out at the eerie landscape. The mist clung to the buildings, so thick that I couldn't see the roads or pavements, and I could barely make out the stalls on the marketplace. Even the clanking of scaffolds and the yakking of stallholders were dulled this morning.

But it wasn't the mist that put me off, rather the thought of being caught off guard by one of the Labyrinthians' many secret henchmen.

"Knock knock!" Ezra's call had spooked me so much I'd thrown half of the hot liquid over myself.

"What are you doing here?" I'd asked as he had apparated in my living room.

"I thought I'd pop by," he'd lied. "See what you've done to the place."

"Not much." I'd traipsed through to the kitchen to refill my mug and clean myself up. I would never get used to not being able to offer him one.

"It's alright, is this." Ezra had given it his seal of approval. "Cosy. Better than where you used to live. That had no character."

"The *landlady* was a character. Didn't that count?" I'd asked.

"No," he'd replied. "She was a capitalist. They have bank accounts instead of characters." Ezra had always complained about the cost of his rent and, as far as I'd known, he'd paid a pittance. I'd never known what he did with his money. Maybe he used to give it all away to his informants. That would be just like him.

"Are we going?" he'd asked.

"I haven't even had a shower yet," I'd grumbled.

"No time like the present," he'd said and hurried me along.

Now we'd arrived at the office and he floated up the stairs ahead of me. Easily navigating stairs had to be a perk of being dead.

"Sometimes you need a chaperone," Ezra told me. "I'm not keen to have you spirit-side too soon."

"Arrr, that's nice." I smiled. "Looking out for me."

"Looking out for myself. I couldn't bear the nagging."

"Oh, fine," I huffed.

The office was surprisingly busy. Wootton was organising piles of paper, and Snitch—who you rarely saw at this time of day—was on his knees fiddling with the printer.

Even Dodo was awake and appeared to be directing matters.

"What's going on?" I asked, dropping my bag beside my chair and unbuttoning my raincoat. It would take a week for my leather jacket to recover after being caught in the deluge yesterday. I'd left it to dry and air out on the back of a chair at home.

"Wizard Dodo, may his heart be forever blessed," Wootton said, and I had the impression he didn't really mean that, "took it upon himself to do some research last night and rather overdid it."

I regarded the piles of paper on the floor in wonder. "I didn't know we had this much printing paper in the stock cupboard," I marvelled.

"We didn't," Wootton confirmed.

"Not much point in being a wizard if you can't replace your own paper, is there?" Dodo asked. "It's magick paper. It saves trees."

"I don't really fink you needed to print out half a dozen copies of everything, Wizard Dodo," Snitch told him.

"I thought everyone would want to see what I'd found out," Dodo replied.

"And what did you find out?" Ezra asked as I bent down to pick up a stack and flick through it.

"Absolutely nothing." Dodo shrugged. "Must have smoked too much of that whacky—"

"Is that what you were smoking?" I recoiled in horror. "Please don't repeat that in front of DCI Wyld."

"Why not?" The old wizard's eyes lit up. "I'm dead. He can hardly arrest me now, can he?"

He and Ezra chuckled away together like a pair of co-

conspirators. Another benefit of being dead, I suppose. I dumped the pile of paper I was holding into the wastepaper bin.

"I finks somefin is jammed in 'ere," Snitch said, and he sounded happy too. "I might have to take it apart."

"Good goddess," I said, under my breath. "There really isn't going to be enough coffee for this shizazz."

The phone on Wootton's desk began to shrill. He looked up from his stacks of nonsensical wizard research. "Would you mind getting that, boss?"

I tutted. "Of course not. Do I have to make my own coffee too?"

"Unless you mind waiting a minute or four," Wootton said.

Reaching over, I plucked the receiver from its cradle, lyrically chanting, "Good morning! Wonderland Detective Agency, Elise Liddell speaking. How may I assist you?"

"DI Liddell?" a female voice repeated.

"Yes. Can I help you?"

"Sandra Rathbone here from Assistant Chief Constable Wiley's office."

Wiley. One of the topmost bosses at the MOWPD.

"Hello." I didn't know what else to say.

"ACC Wiley is sorry to trouble you at this time of day, but he would very much appreciate it if you would be able to meet with him this morning," Sandra said.

Ooh. Now, *this* was interesting. "May I ask what the meeting's concerning?"

"I'd rather not say on the telephone," Sandra said, sounding genuinely apologetic.

"I can probably fit you in," I said, knowing full well that

my diary was empty for the whole day. All I had on my plate were eight murders, one attempted murder and a missing MOWPD Dark Squad officer.

"You're too kind," Sandra replied smoothly. "ACC Wiley can see you at nine."

Back when I'd been serving with the MOWPD, I had never seen inside the assistant chief constable's office. On the half dozen occasions I'd received commendations, they had all taken place on the homicide floor in the basement, surrounded by my friends and colleagues. Our offices were jammed full of desks piled high with case files and filing cabinets to keep them in. Even after we had supposedly gone paperless, we'd generated enough waste to power a small city.

The walls had been covered in photos of both victims and suspects and crime scenes, some of them so heinous, you could hardly bear to look at them. Alongside these were innocuous reminders printed out by administrators or some of our primmer colleagues. *Please remember to turn off the fan when you leave. Please remember to put your phone on call direct when you leave for the day.* Or in the kitchen, *Colleagues are not here to clean up your mess! Please label the food you place in the fridge. Please do not reheat fish in the microwave.*

But ACC Wiley didn't enjoy any of those luxuries.

He had access to an enormous suite of rooms, including offices for the people he kept around him, Sandra Rathbone being one of three administrators, as well as a large meeting room and a comfortable office of his own. The entire floor, shared between him and his two deputies, had been furnished in creams and soft browns and blues. Cream on the walls, brown on the floors, blue seats, brown and blue touches. Large photographs of Tumble Town through the years hung on the walls. The overall effect was calming, and yet the anonymous sterility of it almost made me anxious.

Sandra met me at the lift and shepherded me through to his office. When she offered to take my raincoat, I let her and self-consciously smoothed my damp hair and wiped my hands on my jeans. Had I known I'd be meeting the Big Boss himself today, I'd have dressed with more care.

And if Ezra hadn't been in such a tearing hurry ...

"DI Liddell?" ACC Wiley flung the door of his inner sanctum wide open so that I could step inside. He was a tall man, about six foot two, with close-cropped silver hair. His face had a pleasant set to it, with wide grey eyes and a strong jaw. He was clean shaven—in fact, everything about him was clean. His shirt was freshly pressed; even his tie looked as though it might be fresh out of cellophane. I judged him to be in his early fifties, but he was fit with a broad chest and I suspected, from the size of his upper arms, he liked to lift weights.

"Is Sandra looking after you?" he asked, indicating a chair in front of his desk.

"Oh, I'm fine, sir," I said. "I haven't long had break-fast." That was a lie. So far I'd had half a mug and a couple of swallows of coffee. "Thank you, though."

"And thank you for seeing me at such short notice. I appreciate you're a busy woman." He sat down opposite me and picked up a manilla folder.

Aye, aye, I thought. *Not the old manilla folder. All there is to know about Elise Liddell.*

"The Wonderland Detective Agency, isn't it?"

"That's right, sir," I answered, wondering when we'd get to the point of this meeting.

"How did you come up with that name?" ACC Wiley asked, his eyes raking my face.

"A sudden flash of inspiration." I smiled. "On account of a number of coincidences. My landlady loves Alice in Wonderland and makes a living from creating distinctive top hats. Liddell also happens to be the real surname of the little girl that Lewis Carroll based his character on."

"Fascinating," Wiley said, studying the notes in his folder once more. "But you are a sad loss to the force."

"Well, thank you, sir," I replied, genuinely touched.

"I understand you work closely with DCI Wyld?"

Hmm. Now I had to be careful. It wouldn't do to insinuate that Wyld shared information with me. That would be against MOWPD protocol and get him into some serious hot water. "In the course of my investigations, if I find anything pertinent to any of his cases, I am happy to pass it on," I said.

And, of course, that was true.

"And?" Wiley waited, his grey eyes appraising me.

"And ..." I took a breath. "Occasionally I do some investigative work on his behalf, answering to him. Gratis," I added, just in case there were any issues with payment for that kind of work.

"Mmm." Wiley's response was non-committal. "And apparently you're friendly with Cerys Pritchard?"

Ah-ha! That's what this meeting was about. Monkton

had fed Pritchard's request up the line and it had reached all the way to the top. Impressively quickly.

"We were colleagues," I told him. "We worked together for about five years, six maybe. We were never close, but we did go out after our shifts sometimes. The whole team did," I explained.

"So you wouldn't say you were her confidant?"

I searched back through the fog of time and the blurred years when I had been working and drinking and burning the candle at both ends. "I suppose she confided in me from time to time, and I in her on occasion. Mostly about relationships."

But then I thought of Makepeace. Initially, I remembered him as the young newcomer on the team. Then I recalled how he'd looked when I found him in the yard behind the disused factory on Tudor Lane. My blood ran cold.

"Not all relationships," I clarified. "In fact, no. I really didn't know her well." I'd had no idea about Makepeace. No idea she'd been working for an underground organisation. "And I don't understand why she did what she did."

Wiley nodded. Perhaps this satisfied him. Nonetheless he continued, "Yet despite this, Pritchard insists she will only communicate through you."

I shifted in my chair and knotted my fingers together in my lap. "That's not of my doing, sir."

"No, no. I realise this." He waved my protestation away. "Her recent demand to be relocated from The Hawthorn West Hospital for the Criminally Insane has been forwarded to me."

"I know it's ridiculous—"

"And yet, perhaps it isn't." Wiley's eyes bore into mine. "Pritchard is sitting on information that is invaluable to the MOWPD."

"Yes, but—"

"And not only homicide. There are a number of teams interested in what she has to say and what she can tell us about the Labyrinthians, especially with regard to Superintendent Ibeus's role within that organisation. The Serious Crime team, for example. Organised crime. Fraud. The Dark Squad. The Labyrinthians have tentacles in far too many dark holes. Imagine our clear-up rate if we could trace the person behind all of this and put him away."

Or her.

I opened my mouth and closed it again. Where was this going?

"I have taken this to the Ministry of Witches and the Council for the Paranormal. We are agreed that Pritchard will be transferred, as per her request, to Belhus Wood Open Prison."

I shot out of my seat. "With all due respect, ACC Wiley—"

Wiley didn't so much as blink. "Please take a seat, DI Liddell. There's no need to let emotion get the better of you."

"It's not emotion!" I blurted out. "She's psychopathic. Sociopathic. She's incarcerated in a hospital for the criminally insane. She didn't suddenly magick herself sane in the past forty-eight hours!"

"Please." Wiley gestured at my chair once more. "Are you sure I can't offer you some tea?"

"No," I said, but I sat down as he insisted, and released a tense breath. "But thank you."

"You have to understand that our need for this information outweighs any other concerns we might have. To that end, we have arranged Pritchard's transfer to Belhus Wood today."

I gaped at him. "Today?"

He glanced at his watch. "This morning, in fact. That's why I asked you here. We would like you to meet her at Belhus Wood at one this afternoon. She will have had a chance to settle into her new quarters and take a walk around the grounds. The governor, Velma Hadid, is a personal friend of mine and will have outlined all the benefits that serving a sentence at Belhus Wood has to offer. There is a working farm, a stable, a kennel, allotments, a decent library, opportunities for education—even a hair salon and a beauty parlour where the women can receive training but also have treatments."

"Sounds wonderful," I said, struggling to keep the sark from my tone.

"When you meet with Pritchard, you will remind her of her end of the bargain. She must deliver the information to you, then and there. If she doesn't, you will inform her that all privileges will be revoked and we will move her back to Hawthorn West before the sun sets."

Wow.

"We're not playing games here, DI Liddell," Wiley told me with a lift of his chin. "The stakes are high for everyone."

"Am I going in alone?" I asked.

"She swears she will only speak to you." Wiley

shrugged. "Which does not mean, of course, that we won't be recording all that we see and hear."

The room would have cameras and microphones. That made sense.

My mind raced. I didn't like this, not one little bit. There was so much that could go wrong. What if Pritchard had been lying when she said she could give me information? What if she realised we'd called her bluff? What if she went batpoop crazy?

"You'll do it?" Wiley pressed.

I exhaled sharply. "I don't like it, but yes, I'll do it."

"Splendid!" Wiley licked his lips, the cat who got the cream. "And don't worry. You don't have to like it. Once we have what we need, she'll be moved back to Hawthorn West where, the goddess willing, they'll lock her up and throw away the key."

Ouch. I closed my eyes. A double-cross.

The whole thing stank to high heaven.

And I was the messenger.

I could only hope nobody was intending to shoot me.

CHAPTER 18

If Witchity Grubbs was low tech, echoing to the sound of jangling keys and clanking gates, and The Hawthorn West Hospital for the Criminally Insane was high tech, with swooshing doors and eyes in the sky, Belhus Wood Open Prison was something else altogether.

Low security, most of the doors didn't have locks at all. Even the main gates stood open to allow people to pass through, both coming and going. Sure, someone was keeping a vague eye on things, but for the most part, Belhus Wood looked to all intents and purposes like a rambling housing estate with a limited number of houses.

Here, outside London, there was no mist. I'd left that behind in Tumble Town. Instead, the sky was a pale, dusky blue, the clouds heavy and white with grey around the edges, promising rain later. As we approached the vicinity of Belhus Wood, I stared around at the countryside. Everywhere I looked there were parties of women in bright yellow vests working. Pruning, planting, trimming, sweeping, fixing fences, mending walls. They chatted and laughed together, and even with the car windows tightly shut, I could tell some were singing.

They were happy.

Belhus Wood was a place where witches could unlock some potential. They would serve short sentences and, on release, would take their place back in the world—in Tumble Town or wherever else that might be—and live fulfilling lives.

In theory at least.

Not Cerys though. Wiley had seen to that. He would milk her of any information she had and then he'd personally ensure she would never see the light of day again.

I shouldn't have cared.

But I didn't like the duplicity of it all. There had to be other ways and means.

"Penny for them?" Monkton asked. Funnily enough, he'd drawn the short straw—or he'd volunteered, not that he'd admit it—and was driving me to Belhus Wood. I could have driven myself, but I didn't have a car and I was no longer insured to drive the police pool ones. There hadn't been time to organise a rental.

"I'm not sure they're worth that much," I told him.

"You're just going to have to distance yourself from it," Monkton said, not unkindly. He'd been briefed on what was happening. Perhaps the powers that be imagined he'd be able to exert more control over me than they could. They were probably right. I wasn't beholden to them. Not anymore. But I respected Monkton far too much to do the dirty on him.

"Get in. Do the job. Get out," he continued. "You

know as well as I do that Hawthorn West is the best place for her."

"Yes, I know," I murmured.

"You have to play it cool, Elise. She'll twig otherwise."

"I know."

"And think what we can do with the information she has—"

"I know, I know!" I said, wishing he'd shut up.

He laughed. "Then pull yourself together."

We drove along a lane; no potholes here. No doubt they'd been filled in by the residents. Every building we encountered had a square, cream sign with a green number printed on it. We were looking for number 13.

Unlucky for some, I thought, as Monkton pointed it out. There were no parking bays, so he pulled up directly outside. "I'll be waiting here," he told me, offering a reassuring pat on my arm as I hauled myself out of the car.

"I have no idea how long I'll be," I told him, depositing my handbag on the passenger seat and reaching into the well for the file Wiley had prepared for me.

He yawned. "I'll listen to some jazz." He turned on the radio and slouched down in his seat. Give him two minutes and he'd be asleep.

I approached the door of number 13 with some trepidation, unsure what I'd find. It looked like the front door you'd see on any country cottage. There was no bell or buzzer. I wasn't sure whether to knock or walk straight in. In the end, I did the latter.

Inside there was a reception of sorts. At a desk, close to the door, a woman in a bright yellow jumper with a green and cream lanyard beamed up at me from her swivel seat.

The ever-present computer screen dominated the desk, along with a pile of envelopes. She was busy stuffing paper into them for a mailshot of some kind. Behind her, scruffy mismatched chairs were arranged around the walls. A couple of people were waiting there. One man regarded me with curiosity. The other, a woman my age, chewed on her thumbnail and watched the second hand go round on the wall clock.

"Good afternoon!" the woman at the desk sang. "Do you have an appointment?"

"I'm Elise Liddell," I said, drawing my wallet out of my pocket. "I'm here to see Cerys Pritchard."

"Pritchard?" the woman repeated and scrolled through the page on her screen. "Oh yes. Transferred just this morning! Awesome. Take a seat. I'll let them know you're here."

It wasn't immediately clear to me who 'them' might be, but for the sake of argument I chose to assume it was the governor and maybe a security officer.

I sat beneath the wall clock and immediately regretted doing so, because now, not only was the curious man watching me, but also the woman with the tatty thumbnail. I tried not to feel self-conscious, but failed.

Fortunately, I didn't have to wait long. Within four minutes, a door opened and a man with a straggly beard and round glasses stared out into the waiting room. "Ms Liddell?" he asked.

I nodded and stood.

"I'm Dave Lexington, one of the officers here."

"Hi." I was taken aback. He looked like he'd be at home working in a library or for social services, not as a prison officer.

"This way." He moved away from the door, indicating I should follow him. We climbed a narrow stretch of stairs and passed through a fire door onto a corridor. The building was larger inside than I'd imagined. There were half a dozen doors on this floor, although it occurred to me that the space had been partitioned. There would have been fewer rooms originally, and they would have been larger.

"Ms Pritchard is waiting for you in room 6," the man told me.

"How is she?" I asked.

"Quiet," he said.

"Unresponsive?" I asked, knowing that she'd rarely spoken to anyone during her previous incarcerations.

"Civilised, but not particularly forthcoming," came the slightly guarded reply.

"But she's not causing any problems?" I checked.

"None at all."

"And is she secured?"

"Secured?" The man blinked at me owlishly.

"Handcuffs? Leg cuffs?"

"Good goddess, no!" The very idea appalled him. "We don't do that at Belhus Wood."

"Ha." *Alrighty then.* "Of course you don't."

"Room 6 is the one at the very end."

"You're not coming in?"

"No, no. I'll let you have your privacy."

❧ ——————

She was standing in front of the open window, her shoulders rolled back. She looked younger than when I'd seen her the previous day. Her face was less lined, perhaps. But the lighting and the colour of the walls—a soft green— were kinder. Less harsh than at Hawthorn West. It did her a few favours.

The room—not a cell—was clean and sparsely furnished. A table with two chairs. A pair of chairs stacked against the wall. A small sofa pushed below the window. As I stepped into the room, she turned and offered the briefest of smiles. "You work wonders, Elise. I knew you would." Even her voice had lost its brittle edge.

"I really don't think any of this is down to me," I told her. "I passed your message on. Someone, somewhere, thought it was a good idea to listen to what you had to say."

"You don't, though?" she asked, zoning in on my discomfort. This is the problem with detectives. They instinctively pick up on every little tell.

I deflected attention by slapping down Wiley's file on the table. It contained an agreement between the Ministry of Witches High Court and Cerys. She would receive a partial pardon for her part in the murder of Wizard Elryn Dodo. The terms of her incarceration would be down-graded, although her life term would still mean a minimum of twenty-five years. She would be eligible to serve out her time at Category C and Open prisons.

It was a complete load of horse manure.

"Is that what I think it is?" Cerys turned to look. "My promise of a room with a view for the rest of my sentence?"

"In return for the information you promised." I took a seat, wanting to get this whole thing over with, and placed my notebook and pencil on top of the file.

"It's a life-changing deal," she said.

I placed my hand over the pile. "It is. You have to sign it before we begin."

She strolled over and gently pulled the file from beneath my clammy palm. Her lips curled up again as she pulled the contents free. Half a dozen sides of closely typed, meaningless drivel. They'd wanted to make it look genuine.

She took a seat opposite me and began to read, slowly and carefully. Occasionally she would glance up and smile politely.

"What's the catch?" she asked eventually, her voice so low it would be all but inaudible on the recordings, I was sure.

"You have to give us the information today. Before I leave." I made sure mine would be picked up.

She nodded.

"They're categorical about that," I told her, straining to keep my tone neutral. "You need to spill the beans before I leave."

"How long do we have?" She turned her wrist over, pretending to check a watch. She didn't have one, and there was no clock on the wall in here.

"Till four," I said.

"Are they recording us?" She scanned the walls and ceiling. What might have been either smoke detectors or sprinklers strategically placed in the corners of the room were a bit of a giveaway to those in the know.

"They are."

"So you won't need to take notes," she said.

I smiled, a smile that I didn't feel. "I might do that anyway," I told her. "Old habits die hard."

"You're a good detective, Elise," she told me. "I always wanted to be like you."

"I wish you had been more like me and less like you," I ventured. "Then neither of us would be sitting here this afternoon and we could both be getting on with things that really matter in life."

She laughed, genuinely amused. "Catching crooks? Isn't that the end result of what happens here today?"

"Is it?" I shrugged. "Nothing's set in stone yet, and at the moment I'm not catching crooks, I'm only sitting across a table chatting to one."

Something dark crossed her face momentarily, then it was gone, replaced with a cool expression, much more difficult to read. "Let's sign this thing, shall we?"

I took the agreement from her and flicked through it until I found the page where she needed to scrawl her signature. I would countersign it, but only to agree that it had been signed in my presence. *Ha*! Believe me, I'd checked and double-checked *that* clause, and even then I'd had Monkton read it through too.

"Do I sign it in pencil?" she asked, twiddling with the one I'd brought with me.

"Yes," I said, because nobody in their right mind would have given her a ballpoint pen which could be put to numerous uses after being 'misplaced'. I'd seen what had happened to wardens and security officers after such implements had been utilised as weapons.

Mind you, a pencil can make a formidable stabbing tool too.

Not pretty.

She signed her name with a flourish and handed me the pencil.

I signed mine beneath hers, then double-tapped the page. The charcoal of our scratchy pencil marks sparkled momentarily before turning a deep, ineradicable purple.

"Nicely done," Cerys remarked.

Shuffling the papers together to tidy them, I slipped them back into the file and pulled my notebook towards me. "So?"

"So ..." She leaned back in her chair and studied the ceiling. "Let me think about how I want to do this."

"How about I ask you some questions and you provide me with the answers?" I suggested.

"How about you just give me time to think?"

Is this how it's going to be? Fine.

I gave her time.

A lot of time.

She sat there silently, staring up at the ceiling.

Occasionally I shot covert glances her way, but she was so deep inside herself that I doubt I registered.

When she sighed and moved, I sat upright, but she simply climbed to her feet and went to stand in front of the window, her face turned away from me.

"It's quite simple," I said. "I need to know about the Labyrinthians."

She pursed her lips and rotated at the waist to regard me with something akin to pity. "I hate to say this, but you're really not as clever as you would like to think you are."

"I have never defined myself as clever," I told her. "Merely curious."

"Insatiably so, I'd say." She inhaled noisily and turned back to the window. I found myself suddenly fearful that she would crash through it and either do herself irreparable harm or otherwise roll to her feet and disappear into the countryside.

She did neither, merely pressed her forehead against the glass for a long moment.

I was running out of patience. "Were the Labyrinthians behind the murders at Fletcher Gate?"

She lifted a shoulder and twitched, then turned to face me again.

"You made the mistake of assuming that Taurus is one person," she told me.

"She was." I knew that for a fact. "Ibeus was Taurus."

"Was she?"

"She wasn't?" *What is going on here*?

"Taurus is more than one person. Ibeus was a version of Taurus. Not a particularly good one."

This was news to me. Other people who had spoken of Taurus spoke of a single person. "Taurus is ... a group of people?"

"Taurus is a rank. Taurus can be replaced."

I frowned at Cerys. "That's why Ibeus was there. She was eradicated."

Cerys said nothing.

"She outlived her usefulness. She's been replaced." I was thinking out loud now.

Still Cerys did not respond.

"What about the Labyrinthians?" I pushed. "Who's in charge?"

"Is the Ministry of Witches run by a single person?" Cerys countered.

My brain attempted to discern her meaning. The Council of Witches and Wizards were a group of people. The Ministry of Witches referred to an institution but also a much more abstract concept. A historical artefact. Could she be suggesting that the Labyrinthians were some kind of umbrella organisation? Something intangible?

Or was she trying to wrongfoot me?

I tried again. "Was the new Taurus behind the tea party murders?"

She declined to give me a straight answer. "You'd be a bit frustrated if you felt people were ganging up on you, wouldn't you?"

"I might feel frustrated, but I probably wouldn't invite them round to dinner and then poison them all. It's just not polite."

Cerys laughed. "You have no imagination, that's your problem, Elise."

"And the fact that you can't see how wrong it is, is yours," I told her.

She raised her eyebrows. "Touché."

"Time's a-ticking, Cerys. We need something. You know from reading the agreement, if you don't give me anything they can work with, the deal is off."

"Hmm." She placed her palms together in front of her chest, like a little girl praying. "I hear. I see. I feel," she said. Her eyes lost focus and her face paled. For one awful moment I thought she was going to collapse. I pushed my chair back, and the noise it made as it scraped the floor brought her back to her senses.

I stopped in front of her, just a couple of feet between us. "Are you okay?" I asked.

"I gave you my promise," she said.

"So tell me—"

"You wilfully misunderstand. I gave *you* my promise. I would pass what was needed to *you*." She pointed up at the ceiling. "And only to you."

Oh, jeepers. "Cerys—"

"That was my promise."

"You've signed the agreement."

She took a step closer to me. We were almost face to face. We hadn't been this close since the last time I'd seen her in Tudor Lane when we'd swapped pleasantries, even as I was investigating who had killed Wizard Dodo.

"That agreement isn't worth the paper it's written on. You know that. I know that." She wasn't whispering but her voice was low, disturbingly quiet. I had to lean in slightly to hear what she was saying.

"They'll send you back to Hawthorn West."

"They're sending me back anyway. I haven't even been allowed to unpack my belongings. That's a bit of a giveaway."

"Just give us something."

"No." She reached out and touched me just below my right collar bone. I knocked her hand away.

She laughed, soundlessly. "If I had the power to stop someone's heart with a single touch, I would never have needed to stab that old fossil, would I?"

Dodo. "Do you have no remorse?" I asked.

"Remorse is a useless emotion. It can't undo what has been done. Besides, it makes a person weak, Elise. It makes *you* weak."

I couldn't stand to listen to this a moment longer. I

took a step away. She reached out and grabbed my wrist with a grip of iron, tugging me so close that I could have kissed her. Before I could yank my arm away, she whispered, "I promised I'd give *you* something and I will."

She released me, and, unbalanced, I fell back.

"Hey!" She turned her head up and shouted at the cameras, raising her arms in a salute. "Here's my deal! It's the only one I'm going to give you, so listen carefully!" She pivoted in a circle, taking in all corners of the room. "If I remain here, and *only* if I remain here at Belhus Wood, when I'm settled and happy and don't think you'll be double-crossing me, then and only then, when I deem the time to be right and safe for all parties, will I send a message to DI Liddell. She will meet with a representative of Taurus. That will be your way to infiltrate the organisation."

She turned back to me, dropping her voice. "I can't direct you straight to them. It would be like signing my own death warrant."

"How will I know?" I asked, rubbing my wrist.

"You'll know."

CHAPTER 19

L ife went on.

Wiley was apparently furious and, for a while, Monkton was confined to desk duties. Fortunately, that didn't last longer than a few days. The MOWPD was short-staffed at the best of times. They couldn't afford to take one of their best homicide detectives off the street for long.

I was glad about that. I couldn't stand him whinging down the phone to me. He was like a bear with a sore head.

I had imagined that Wiley would take some of his angst out on me, but apparently they couldn't afford to do that either. Cerys had stated that she would arrange a meeting with someone in the Labyrinthians who would provide a way for me to infiltrate the organisation. As dubious as that sounded, that was all we had to go on, and for now, the powers that be let me go about my business without inter-ference.

Meanwhile, Cerys remained at Belhus Wood, enjoying all the freedoms she had ever yearned for. Living the life of luxury while poor dead Dodo lamented the loss of his great grimoire collection, and DC Kevin Makepeace lay mouldering in his grave.

Of course, I couldn't put it behind me. I had no intention of doing so. The files remained permanently open on my computer. Every person I came across was a potential Labyrinthian connection. I had Ezra and Wootton screen clients ahead of meeting with them, and I was more careful than ever while strolling the lanes of Tumble Town.

As for running? I'd almost given that up.

"Any news?" Monkton asked me, nine days after my meeting with Cerys. "Anything I can take back to Wiley?"

We had arranged to meet for dinner at The Full Moon Inn, not far from the Ministry of Witches. They had the best pie and mash this side of the Thames.

"Nothing," I said.

"Maybe she's stringing us along." Monkton was only toying with his cheese and onion pie.

"Of course she is," I grunted. "She enjoys the power."

Monkton pushed his plate away and picked up his glass to wave it at one of the servers. She came across and took his order, then hustled his plate away.

"I'm still eating," I grumbled, mouth full. "Are you in a rush?"

"To get drunk," Monkton told me.

I tapped my glass of sparkling water with my fork. "You're on your own there. What's eating you tonight?"

"Where would I start?"

"Well, obviously. What's bothering you apart from *everything*?"

He drew his notebook out of his pocket and opened it up. "Mickey sent me a full list of the victims from the tea party."

"His team managed to track them all down, eh?"

"Yeah. I don't think it was easy, so all credit to him." He tapped the page. "Seanie Pendlebury. Informant. Fusty Dankcellar. Magistrate."

I lay my knife and fork down.

"Lawrence Whityclaw. Ex-judge."

My appetite had disappeared.

"Wesley Warthog. Informant. Randy Prock. Informant."

I considered ordering a shot of Blue Goblin.

"Megrin Folstrop. Ex-special constable."

Make it two.

"Tobias Tuttlewhirl. Ex-detective. Yvonne Ibeus. Ex-superintendent, MOWPD homicide."

"Rest in peace," I said and, sliding my own plate away, reached for my water.

Monkton nodded at the server as she came back with a fresh pint. "And we don't have anybody for it!"

"I understand your frustration," I consoled him. "Perhaps we should revisit the case. Start at the beginning. Go through everything we have. Talk to Hornswoggler again. And the Thistlebristles."

Monkton nodded and tipped his glass in salute. "Yeah. Yeah. But not tonight, eh? I want to get home. Play the piano. Drink a few more beers."

"What you need is sleep," I told him. "Leave the piano and the beers and just put your jim-jams on."

He raised his eyebrows. "Maybe I don't wear pyjamas."

I covered my ears. "I don't want to know. La-la-la-la-la!"

Laughing, he drained his drink and signalled to the server to fetch the bill. "And I'll have a shot of whisky to finish," he told her.

I began to dig around in my bag for my purse.

"I'll get this," Monkton told me. "The next one is on you."

"If you're sure?" I stood up and began to pull on my jacket. It's what we usually did. Monkton hated splitting bills so we took it in turns to treat the other. "Thanks!"

"Do you want me to walk you home?" he asked, ever the gentleman.

I considered this, more seriously than I would normally have done, but at some stage you do have to start taking responsibility for yourself. "Nah, I'm good," I told him. "I'll call you tomorrow and we'll talk about how and where we'll start going through the tea party case again. Okay?"

"Tomorrow's Sunday, Liddell. I have a day off."

"Is it?" As if he cared. I had no clue what day it was. "I'll call you anyway."

"Yep, do that." The server handed him the wallet with the bill sticking out of one end. He winked at me as I turned away, and I waved.

Outside I turned my collar up against the chill wind. Drizzle was falling, so softly that I could barely feel it. I might not have noticed at all if I hadn't spotted umbrellas up here and there. Celestial Street thronged with shoppers at this time of night. Many of them chatted cheerfully, barging past me on their way inside The Full Moon Inn or heading in the opposite direction towards the larger stores.

I preferred the smaller, independent shops. Their window displays shone and sparkled, full of enticing wares. I meandered for a while, thinking about the names on Monkton's list, until I came to the bookshop. Pausing, I studied the display of colourful book covers, but the TBR pile beside my bed was a towering fiasco, promising to collapse at any moment. When did I have time to read? I went to bed intending to and invariably passed out in three seconds.

Bed!

Yawning, I resisted the urge to pop in and buy a book and instead crossed over the road and headed down Cross Lane into Tumble Town. I bobbed and weaved along the tight, darkened lanes, just like everyone else. The fact that these thoroughfares were busy tonight actually eased some of my anxiety. Surely no-one would approach me at this time of day? Not when the streets were alive with people.

At the point where the lane narrowed the most, and at the moment when I had almost reached my left turn, a large-framed older woman, head swathed in a scarf that knotted beneath several of her chins, hobbled along the lane towards me.

I had nowhere to go.

I squeezed against the building to my left to allow the woman as much room as she needed. Not old by any means, she had a limp that was particularly pronounced. As she drew closer, moving directly into the light of a nearby window, I observed her ruby-red lipstick and false eyelashes. Her cheeks were rouged unnecessarily bright too. She had an appearance akin to some grotesque baby doll, but with deepening lines around her nose, mouth and eyes, and while she didn't look directly at me, I could tell she was sizing me up.

"Good evening," I said as she drew level with me, my only intention to break the awkwardness as she attempted to squeeze past, but she made no such effort to avoid me, and shoulder barged me out of her way.

The force with which she hit me catapulted me backwards. I fought for my footing on the slippery cobblestones, lost the battle and slid to the floor, grazing my knuckles on the wall as I reached for something to break my fall.

She continued relentlessly, stepping over me as I lay prone and winded.

"Do you mind?" I sat up, shaking my hand and spraying droplets of blood around. "Hey!" I scooted round on my backside to give her a piece of my mind ...

But she'd gone!

"Ugh." I pushed myself up to standing, slightly embarrassed by what had happened, then jerked backwards as a shape flew at me.

It hit me on the chest and I grappled with it for a moment before realising it was harmless. An envelope. A bright white rectangle, gleaming and light as a feather. Expensive vellum—starched and crisp, with my name written beautifully across the surface.

"Huh?" I held it in both hands and stared down at it.

A growl rolled out of the darkness, making me jump. "Excuse you."

I whirled. Eyes glared at me from beneath a black hood. Just someone behind me. Wanting to get past.

My nerves were tingling. "Beg your pardon." I hastened along the lane until I came to a crossroads where the light was better and there was more room. I stood beneath a lamp and stared at the envelope. I should open it. See what it said.

I imagined I already had the gist.

With slightly shaking hands, partly from unease, partly because adrenaline had started to kick in, I tore it open. Before I could unfold the paper, my phone began to ring.

I crumpled the note and stuffed it under my arm so I could fish my phone out of the back pocket of my jeans. Monkton.

"Hey—" I said. "You'll never guess—"

"Oh, I bet I will." He sounded pumped.

"You've received one too?"

"Instead of a bill. I stayed for another whisky, and lo and behold, when I went to pay, the bill had turned into another invitation. One I'd be hard pressed to refuse."

"What does yours say?"

"You go first," Monkton said.

"I haven't read mine. Hang about." I tucked the phone between my shoulder and my ear and rescued the letter.

"Dear Elise Liddell," I read.

"The Spiritual Repatriation Society for Dead Witches and Wizards is pleased to announce a memorial for the unfortunate victims of recent Tumble Town homicides.

We would be pleased if you would attend at Fletcher Gate at 10 pm this evening.

Entry is strictly by invitation only.

We look forward to seeing you then.

With all good wishes."

"And then there's a signature I can't read," I finished.

"Exactly the same," Monkton told me. We lapsed into momentary silence, each of us considering our options.

"What now?" I asked.

"Invitation only," he replied. "No backup."

"Yeah. What time is it now?"

"Nine thirty-six."

"If you hurry, you'll just make it," I told him. "I'll wait for you outside."

CHAPTER 20

I stood across the road, waiting for Monkton in the shadows where Snitch must have been hanging out on the night of the tea party. I kept a careful eye on number 48, one ear out for my ex-boss and the other straining to hear anyone else who might approach.

Number 48 was lit up like a Christmas tree, every window radiating warmth.

That in itself was peculiar. Why were the empty rooms upstairs illuminated? Since when had the police released the scene? The investigation was still ongoing, and the owner or owners of the building had not been traced.

As I'd imagined, I heard Monkton before I saw him. He jogged into view a few seconds later, puffing a little. It wasn't that he was unfit, more that he'd had to cover over a mile to get to me, and he was far too old to give Usain Bolt a run for his money.

"Ooof." Monkton pulled up in front of me and ran a hand through his hair. "What gives?"

"Absolutely nothing," I told him. "I've been standing

here for five minutes. No-one has gone in. No-one has come out. I haven't seen the flicker of a shadow."

He checked his watch. "Two minutes to."

I nodded. "Let's go."

Like thieves in the night, we crossed the road and clambered up the stone steps to the front door. Monkton pressed the brass bell and we heard it jangle inside.

Nobody came.

I tried the door. Locked.

Monkton smacked on the wood with the palm of his hand.

Still no answer.

Leaning against the wood, I pressed my ear to the crack. I could hear the faint ticking of the grandfather clock, and even as I listened I could hear it as it wound itself up to start announcing the hour.

Ding-dong, ding-dong. Ding-dong, ding-dong.
Clink.

The lock made a distinct unlatching sound. Monkton reached for the handle.

Bong!

He turned it. And pushed.

Bong!

It was no longer locked.

Bong!

It swung wide.

Bong!

We stared into the elegant hallway. The fire burned in the grate. The portrait above stared down at us.

Bong!

We stepped through. Someone had arranged vases of

flowers on two Roman-style plinths. The cloying smell of vanilla was almost too much for me.

Bong!

A third plinth stood in the centre of the hallway, with a varnished wooden box perched on it. I followed Monkton further inside to take a better look. It was sturdy—

A deafening boom rocked the very foundations of the whole house.

Behind me, the door had slammed shut. I spun, imagining some catastrophe was about to befall us.

Monkton swore under his breath. "Good goddess! That nearly gave me a heart attack."

Reaching for my wand, I turned about, checking in the darker corners, under the stairs and then craning my head to peer up. Nothing. Glancing to my right I could see the door to the library was open, and inside there, the fire was burning too. Before I could go and investigate, Monkton called me back.

"See this?"

There was a note attached to the top of the box. *As a matter of courtesy, please post your wands and phones inside.*

I didn't like it. Not one little bit.

My eyes met Monkton's. "I don't want to do that," I said.

He gave a slight shrug. I wasn't sure what that meant. Maybe he assumed we'd be capable of meeting any challenge without phones and wands.

Perhaps he was right.

Reluctantly, I slid my phone out of my pocket and dropped it into the box. Monkton did the same, followed by his wand. I grudgingly followed suit. There went another wand. "You know there's no way of opening this box?" I asked him.

Monkton tipped his head. First one way and then the other. "Listen."

I did as he suggested, holding my breath, eyes rolling left to right. "I don't hear anything," I whispered.

"Exactly!" He pointed at the grandfather clock. It had stopped. "It didn't get to chime ten—"

"I wasn't counting," I murmured.

A loud scratching began to emanate from the direction of the dining room. We edged in that direction. Before we could reach the door, music began to play. Light. A string quartet or something similar.

"Music for tea parties," Monkton said.

I itched to plunge my hand through the gap in the top of the box to retrieve my wand, but there was no way it would have fit.

Monkton began to stride purposefully towards the dining room. I was having second thoughts, but faint heart never caught ghastly crooks, so I went after him.

He threw open the door, then stood and observed the room. I peered over his shoulder. He'd been right. Another tea party. The furniture had been returned—or perhaps replaced. And the portraits had been rehung on the walls! The table had been set, but this time only for three. Steam rose out of the mismatched teapots. Tiny cakes were arranged on stands. There were sweet little ham sandwiches cut in triangles and small plates of savoury delicacies. Caviar. Smoked trout.

"Ugh," said Monkton, ever the vegetarian.

"There's olives," I pointed out. "And cherry tomatoes."

"I'll pass."

"Fair enough." So would I.

I walked the length of the room to where a gramophone had been set up in the corner. I plucked up the needle to silence the dinky-dinky-dinky-dink. It seemed awfully out of place to me, playing such cheerful, frivolous sounds in a room where eight people had died only a couple of weeks previously.

Silence.

Monkton pointed at the clocks. Each of them had stopped a few seconds after ten. Presumably at the moment we walked in.

Curious.

I checked the door with the stained-glass panels that led into the kitchen. Either it was locked or it had been secured by the police. Wherever the food and drink had come from, it hadn't been prepared on the premises. Not naturally. Just like before.

I'd have rather boiled my head than touched a morsel that had been laid out for us.

Monkton circled the table. "It's set for three," he confirmed. "And—"

"Hello?" A voice, quivering with fear, called out.

I saw Monkton reach for his wand, then frown when he realised he didn't have it.

Yep, I thought. *Exactly*!

"Is there anyone here?" the voice called. I began to walk towards the door as a figure materialised there.

Maizie Thistlebristle.

She blew out a hard breath when she saw me. "Oh, thank goodness."

Honestly? "Why are you here?" I scolded her.

"I have an invitation!" She waved an envelope at me. "To a memorial. It seemed only fitting to come along and say my goodbyes."

She stepped into the room but then noticed Monkton. "Who's this?" she asked, and began to back away again.

"My ex-boss," I told her. "DCI Monkton Wyld. He should have been here that night too." As I said it, the obvious struck me. We were three of the five survivors. Hari was still safe in hospital, recovering. We had no idea where Culpeper was because no-one had heard from him.

But here were we three, all in the murder room together. My stomach sank into my feet. "I think we should leave."

Monkton nodded. "The three of us, invited here—"

"We shouldn't be here," I said. "Not alone."

Bong!

Maizie smiled and stepped back into the doorway. "I'm sorry," she said. "But you can't leave. I'm under strict instructions—"

Bong!

The clocks in the room had started up again. All of them were in perfect synchronicity. Wheels turning, pendulums swinging, second hands ticking. I spun in confusion, hearing a hiss. To my horror, I spied white spray spewing out of the centre of each clock face.

"Gas!" I shrieked.

Monkton made a run for the door, but Maizie disappeared through it and slammed it closed in her wake.

Monkton grabbed the door handle and pulled with all his might. The brass fixings shattered in his hand, as though made of glass. With nothing to pull on, he fell backwards into me. I didn't have time to get out of his way. We tumbled to the floor.

He flipped over onto his front. "We need to stay low," he told me, crawling towards the table. "We'll use the table-cloth to cover our faces."

But even as he reached for the cloth, I noted the way the gas sank. I took a shallow breath, willing myself to stay calm. The slightest breath tickled the back of my throat. Involuntarily, I began to cough. My eyes started to stream. Monkton gagged and began to retch. I remained on my belly, slithering along the floor, reaching for him, but the muscles in my arms and legs were turning to jelly, the strength in my core failing me. I couldn't catch my breath. I panted, in desperate need of air ...

Monkton pulled on the table cloth and cowered as everything fell, showering him in cutlery and glasses, food and drink. Teapots shattered, liquid splashed around us, cakes rolled across the floor. I averted my eyes to avoid flying shards and then turned back to him but, as I did so, another movement caught my eye. I glanced up, my gaze locking on the portrait of the witch above the fire. Her features much the same as Cerys's.

How come I hadn't noticed that before?

The lips were moving. Surely I was hallucinating. "Time's a-ticking, Elise," she seemed to say. "Isn't that what you told me? Time's a-ticking!" And then she laughed with chilling glee.

"You don't get to call the shots," I wheezed, and aimed a direct beam of defensive energy at the portrait using only my hand. It wouldn't have harmed a human, perhaps merely disabling them. Something akin to a taser. But the portrait had been forged from wood, canvas and inflammable oil paint. It burst into flames. Destroying it wouldn't harm Cerys herself and didn't mean anything beyond being a symbolic and ultimately futile gesture of my angst, but it gave me the satisfaction of knowing that she couldn't watch me die.

"I'm not a bloody spectator sport," I growled, and began clawing my way to the rear door and the entrance to the kitchen. I knew the door was locked, but perhaps it hadn't been secured in the same way as the ones at the front. I reached up, my stomach spasming in pain with the effort of doing so, and rattled the handle. This one didn't shatter in my grasp.

Then Monkton was beside me, his mouth and nose covered in pretty peach linen. "We ... need to ... break that ... window," he rasped, handing me an elegantly folded napkin before promptly doubling over in agony and throwing up.

Nice.

I tied the napkin around my face with some difficulty and mopped my eyes, feeling my strength ebbing away. We were running out of time. I stood, legs wobbling, and side-stepped poor stricken Monkton so I could hoist the gramophone, the nearest heavy item to hand. I would have one chance at this, and one only. I lurched towards the door, a modern-day Bride of Frankenstein, barely able to see, my stomach griping in agony, and, closing my eyes, positioned myself next to the lock. Gritting my teeth, I threw the gramophone forward. Without the strength to let go, I simply allowed myself to topple with it.

There was a splintering of wood, the cracking of glass, an explosion—or so it seemed—and the world gave way. I fell into darkness, tumbling down a couple of steps and landing on the cool floor.

"Monkton!" I gasped, "Monkton! There's air down here. There's air!"

CHAPTER 21

Twelve hours later, Monkton and I were huddled together on the comfy seats back at the Wonderland office.

"Oh, you poor things!" Hattie was in a flap. "Let me make you some more tea. Are you sure you don't want something to eat?"

Monkton gagged.

"Gracious me, no. Thanks though, Hattie," I said, nudging Monkton with my knee. We'd both spent half the night vomiting into buckets at the hospital. In between times, we'd had water syringed and swilled in almost every orifice in an attempt to clear us of any residue, before eventually being permitted a shower. Now we were bedraggled, with wet hair, wearing police issue jumpsuits loaned to us by the custody sergeant at MOWPD, a personal friend of Monkton's, and our insides felt as though they'd been run through a mechanical cheese grater.

"Thank goodness you'd already called for backup," Wootton said. He was boggle-eyed at all that had gone on.

"Wyld's First Law of Detection," said Ezra. "If someone says, 'come alone', don't."

Monkton nodded. "And my Second Law is, if they tell you not to bring backup, have the whole force on standby."

"Maybe that should be extended to Wyld's Third Law," I suggested. "If someone tells you to abandon your wand, just don't."

Monkton sniffed. His eyes were red raw and he looked, from a distance, as though he had a bad cold. I'm certain I looked no better, but I hadn't studied myself in a mirror. "We'd never have made it through the door had we been armed."

The man was out of his mind. "There was no point going through the door at all!" I argued. "We were stitched up!"

"Like kippers," Ezra agreed.

"How do you stitch a kipper?" Snitch asked. I hadn't even seen him, but there he was, in his place on the floor next to Wizard Dodo, tiny electronic gadget in his hand. Two mornings in a row. Was this becoming a habit?

"Very carefully," Ezra told him, in all seriousness.

Dodo harrumphed. It might have been amusement.

"They were trying to finish you off," Wootton said, his hair standing on end.

Snitch agreed. "Because they didn't get you the first time."

"Well, they didn't get us the second time either," I said, trying to rally the troops.

"Three's the charm," Monkton grumbled.

I needed to be firm. "Then we have to get them before they get us." I shrugged off the blanket Hattie had thoughtfully provided and stood up. There wasn't a great deal of room to pace in the office, but I felt the need to do so. At the very least, my poor sticky lungs needed a workout.

"Think about it. We now know that Ibeus has been replaced. The Labyrinthians operate like a society. That means they probably have multiple leaders. Perhaps some sort of council. We can start digging and see what shows up. Businesses that are linked to anyone who has gained from known crimes that have in turn been linked to Taurus—meaning Ibeus or anyone similar—or their operations." I was rambling, but I didn't care. Wootton began to take notes.

"Organisations that might benefit from being recipients of articles from Wizard Dodo's collection." I nodded at him.

"I can help you with that!" Dodo said. "Then we can hunt everything down again! And this time, I'll destroy it all!"

"We need to find Maizie Thistlebristle and her brother Merlon as a matter of urgency." I jabbed a finger at Monkton. "That's your job."

"Right." He still looked miserable.

"Cerys said she would deliver a link to the Labyrinthians, and she did what she said," I reminded him. "Maizie. We have to find her!"

"It's just unfortunate she didn't mention that the person she'd introduce would try and take us both out at the same time."

"Perhaps we should have expected that," I said, but I hadn't for a moment thought Cerys had the power to arrange that. Not from inside. But all that, 'I hear, I feel, I see' nonsense. Was that her conversing with someone? Some long-range telepathy? What about Dave-the-hippie Lexington?

"We should take a long hard look at every single thing Cerys has ever done and *all* of her contacts," I said. "I imagined she was being manipulated in some way to do the things she did, and now I'm wondering whether we underestimated her."

"I'm sure we did," Monkton said, and Ezra, sitting behind him, nodded an emphatic yes.

"She fooled us all," he said.

"Well, at least we know where she is and how to access her," I said. "Perhaps we can get clearance to go over later today."

The phone on Wootton's desk began its familiar shrill ringing. The noise went right through me. My brain vibrated, nausea washing over me once more.

"Yes. Yes, he is," said Wootton. "DCI Wyld? It's for you. ACC Wiley."

Monkton threw off his blanket, jumped to attention, and hurried over to take the receiver from Wootton.

"Wyld?" He listened. "Yes, sir?" he said. "Much better, sir. Yes, it was an interesting experience. Yes, sir. What?" The remaining colour, not that there was much of it, leached from his face. "No. Yes, sir. Yes, sir. I'll be right on it."

He handed the phone back to Wootton, turned to face me and swallowed hard. I genuinely thought he might pass out.

"What was that you were saying?" he asked.

Puzzled, I stared back at him. "What do you mean?

About Cerys? About ..." I hesitated. "Knowing where she is?"

"We don't," he told me, his eyes hard. "Not any more. She escaped from Belhus Wood this morning, just before dawn. They have search parties out, but you know and I know—"

"She's long gone," I said.

EPILOGUE

S hards of broken china clinked lightly, scattering as I
  entered the hallway and kicked through them.

48 Fletcher Gate.

I'd stood outside for a good ten minutes, sheltering
from the drizzle, listening and watching the property.
Nothing had stirred within. It no longer glowed with light.
It was shuttered and empty and lifeless.

The search for Cerys had proved fruitless thus far. She'd
had it all planned out, hadn't she? I'd been the mouse in her
carefully placed trap. Knowledge about the Labyrinthians
had been the cheese. The transfer to Belhus Wood had
given her the freedom she needed to instigate her escape.

Just what had ACC Wiley been thinking?

Unless he was in on it, of course.

It had come to this. I no longer knew who to trust at
the MOWPD. With the exception of Monkton. He was as
furious as I was. Cerys had told me Taurus had been
replaced. It hadn't occurred to me initially that she meant

the Labyrinthians had installed a new Taurus in the MOWPD.

A new, probably senior-ranking officer, shedding secrets.

"Hey." Minsk pitter-pattered into the hallway behind me.

"Watch out for glass," I said, extracting my—new—phone from my raincoat pocket and lighting up the torch app. "Do you want me to carry you?"

"Do you want me to turn you into a beefburger?" she responded tartly.

I hid a smile. "See all this?" I gestured at the walls where the wallpaper was beginning to come down. Plaster had fallen away from the ceiling, and floor tiles had lifted. The vases lay smashed on the floor and dead flowers were scattered around. The portrait above the fireplace had been slashed down the middle and hung on the wonk. Only the beautiful grandfather clock remained untouched. I eyed it suspiciously, but the hands were set to midnight, and there was no suggestion it would suddenly burst into life. "Only two days ago, this place was pristine."

"The door was unlocked?" Minsk asked, glancing back over her shoulder.

"It was. I walked right in."

"Did the police leave it like that?"

"I doubt they left it unsecured."

"No." Minsk's little nose began working overtime. "So many people—" she said.

"Pardon me?"

She sighed heavily. "The scent of so many people."

"The police, paramedics ... the place was swarming with

them the night they pulled us out of here." And thank the goddess for them.

"And dead people," Minsk continued. "I can smell them too."

"You're in a morbid frame of mind tonight," I told her. "Eight in the dining room." I pointed at the door, half open, the wood splintered where the police had broken through it to rescue me and Monkton.

"More than eight people have died in this house," Minsk told me, hopping through to the dining room. "We're talking dozens. Dozens and dozens."

Reluctantly, I followed her, but I remained half in and half out of the dining room, one foot planted in the hall-way, surveying the wreckage from a safe distance. Much like the hall, this room had been trashed. I stared at the space above the fireplace where the portrait had been hanging, goading me as I began to die.

Well, I didn't die. So there!

"It stinks to high heaven in here," Minsk said. She had a super-sensitive nose. I couldn't smell anything particular, not the way I had the first time I'd opened this door.

I studied the clocks. As with the one in the hall, none of these had been touched. The hands—hour, minute and second—were clasped together at midnight, praying to some higher demonic being, no doubt.

I shuddered, took a breath and stepped back into the hallway.

Minsk followed me.

"What did you want to show me?" she asked.

"This way." I pushed open the door into the library, steeling myself, half expecting the fire to be blazing in here.

It wasn't, though.

Books lay scattered across the floor, spines broken, covers ripped away. The doors that had protected the bookshelves had been wrenched away from their hinges, the glass smashed to smithereens.

Minsk came in after me, lifting her paws high and treading gingerly. I didn't offer to carry her again.

"There's something about this mirror," I told her. "Something odd."

"It doesn't come off the wall?" she asked.

"According to DCI Wyld, it's bound to the building."

"Hmm." She stared up at it, her whiskers twitching.

"We haven't been able to track down the building's proprietors probably because it's been owned—or rather, there's been a building on this site—for over a thousand years. Possibly since London was a grubby little village in the marsh. We've gathered up all the invitations that we have access to, and every single one was sent by an organisation that could feasibly exist, or sounds a lot like one that does exist—including The Esteemed High Society for the Endowment of Judicial Awards—but they only lead us to dead ends."

"But not the same dead end?" Minsk asked, hopefully.

I knew exactly what she was driving at. "No. No links between them. The paper and envelopes are excellent quality but can be purchased in bulk. The handwriting gave us no lead, and the forensic team DCI Wyld has working on that are examining the possibility that it's been magickly formulated rather than written by a person."

"It goes without saying there's no DNA, I suppose?"

"You suppose right."

"What else do you have?" Minsk asked.

"So little." I sighed. "Everyone who was invited to the tea party had either crossed the Labyrinthians at some time, or, like Ibeus and Dankcellar, had become expendable. Besides that, Wootton took a good look at the clocks and the time each stopped using photos and videos from the crime scenes. Our best guess is that each clock had been magickly connected in some way to a particular victim, and they stopped when their victim died. That's why there were only seconds difference between each clock."

"Ooh. That's grim."

I couldn't agree more.

"These people are good," Minsk murmured. "Dangerously good."

"I fell hook, line and sinker for Maizie's story," I lamented. "I genuinely believed her."

"It happens to us all." Minsk attempted to console me —rather gracious in the circumstances.

"But there is one aspect of her story that stands out to me," I said, stepping closer to the mirror. "She told us about seeing someone—someone who matched Culpeper's description—in this room, looking in this mirror."

"You think it's a portal?"

"I'm convinced of it. The forensic team say it isn't. Ezra says it isn't."

"But Elise says it is." Minsk stared up at it thoughtfully.

"What if that aspect of Maizie's story was true?"

Minsk narrowed her beautiful brown eyes. "She lied about everything else."

"And I think she lied about her ooze," I agreed. "Far too fanciful. It's just ..." I stumbled over my words. "Culpeper had an invitation. We know he didn't make it into the dining room, because Hornswoggler didn't see him. What if—" I started to warm to my theme. "What if Culpeper arrived and, like Wyld and I did, came in here first?"

"And the mirror ate him?" Minsk asked, and I think she was only half joking.

"I know this is pie in the sky," I said. "But if this *is* a portal, what if he found a way in? Through the mirror? He isn't dead, not as far as we know, because we've both heard from him."

Minsk's eyes began to shine. "It would be just like him to go where others fear to tread."

"Exactly!"

I reached out and tapped the mirror gently with my finger. Ripples radiated away from the place I'd touched, as though I'd disturbed a pool of still water.

I caught my breath and tried it again. The same thing happened.

"Whoa," Minsk exclaimed.

I tapped a little harder. The mirror was solid, and this time, there were no ripples, only a greasy smudge from my finger.

I tried again, this time more softly than before, and the surface wrinkled as tiny waves emanated from the centre to the gilt edges. When I took my finger away, water dripped from it.

Minsk moved quickly to stand beneath me, catching one of the drips on her tongue.

"Careful!" I cried in alarm.

"It's salty ..." she said. "Like the sea. Do it again."

I smoothed my finger over the mirror, the slightest of

touches. The water undulated. I offered Minsk a dip, then placed my damp finger on my tongue.

"It tastes ... like ... tears," Minsk announced.

My mouth dropped open. "That's it! That's what this is!"

Minsk reared up on her haunches. "The Pool of Tears!"

"And Culpeper is somewhere inside!"

The Wonderland Detective Agency Continues

The Pool of Tears: Wonderland Detective Agency Book 6

In London's creepy underworld, no-one can hear you die!

Following the tragic events at a recent tea party, private investigator and ex-Ministry of Witches Detective Elise Liddell, has more than enough on her plate. With Dodo's library of black and grisly grimoires missing, a manipulative and malevolent murderer on the loose and the disappearance of the Dark Squad's boss, she isn't sure which way to turn.

But one thing is as clear as crystal. If Elise is to make any progress on her open cases, she'll need to venture through the looking glass.

Can Elise find the answers or will everything end in a Pool of Tears?

Also by Jeannie Wycherley

The Complete Wonky Inn Series (in chronological reading order)

The Wonkiest Witch: Wonky Inn Book 1

The Ghosts of Wonky Inn: Wonky Inn Book 2

Weird Wedding at Wonky Inn: Wonky Inn Book 3

The Witch Who Killed Christmas: Wonky Inn Christmas Special

Fearful Fortunes and Terrible Tarot: Wonky Inn Book 4

The Mystery of the Marsh Malaise: Wonky Inn Book 5

The Mysterious Mr Wylie: Wonky Inn Book 6

The Great Witchy Cake Off: Wonky Inn Book 7

Vengeful Vampire at Wonky Inn: Wonky Inn Book 8

Witching in a Winter Wonkyland: A Wonky Inn Christmas Cozy Special

A Gaggle of Ghastly Grandmamas: Wonky Inn Book 9

Magic, Murder and a Movie Star: Wonky Inn Book 10

O' Witchy Town of Whittlecombe: A Wonky Inn Christmas Cozy Special

Judge, Jury and Jailhouse Rockcakes: Wonky Inn Book 11

A Midsummer Night's Wonky: Wonky Inn Book 12

Halloween Heebie-Geebies: Wonky Inn Book 13

Owl I want for Witchmas is Hoo: A Wonky Inn Christmas Cozy Mystery

Oh Mummy!: Wonky Inn Book 14

Pieces of Hate: Wonky Inn Book 15

The Faery of Witchmas Past: A Wonky Inn Christmas Cozy
Special (Release date TBC)

A Barbarous Band of Blood Brothers: Wonky Inn Book 16
(Release date 2023 TBC)

Spellbound Hound

Ain't Nothing but a Pound Dog: Spellbound Hound Magic and
Mystery Book 1

A Curse, a Coven and a Canine: Spellbound Hound Magic and
Mystery Book 2

Bark Side of the Moon: Spellbound Hound Magic and Mystery
Book 3

Master of Puppies: Spellbound Hound Magic and Mystery
Book 4

Up, Pup and Away: Spellbound Hound Magic and Mystery
Book 5 (Release date 2023 TBC)

Wonderland Detective Agency

Dead as a Dodo: Wonderland Detective Agency Book 1

The Rabbit Hole Murders: Wonderland Detective Agency
Book 2

Tweedledumb and Tweedledie: Wonderland Detective Agency
Book 3

The Curious Incident at the Pig and Pepper: Wonderland
Detective Agency Book 4

A Tragic Tea Party: Wonderland Detective Agency Book 5

The Pool of Tears: Wonderland Detective Agency Book 6

Standalones

The Municipality of Lost Souls

Midnight Garden: The Extra Ordinary World Novella Series Book 1

Beyond the Veil

Crone

A Concerto for the Dead and Dying

Deadly Encounters: A collection of short stories

Keepers of the Flame: A love story

Non-Fiction

Losing my best Friend

Thoughtful support for those affected by dog bereavement or pet loss

Follow Jeannie Wycherley

Find out more at on the website

www.jeanniewycherley.co.uk

Have a laugh at Jeannie's Tiktoks

www.tiktok.com/@jeanniewycherley

Or visit her on Facebook for her fiction

www.facebook.com/jeanniewycherley

Follow Jeannie on Instagram (for bears and books)

www.instagram.com/jeanniewycherley

Sign up for Jeannie's newsletter on her website

www.subscribepage.com/JeannieWycherleyWonky

Buy Jeannie a coffee!

www.buymeacoffee.com/jeanniewych

Printed in Great Britain
by Amazon

26798399R00162